SIGNED, SEALED & DEADLY

by Bella Colby

Beresford
Publishing
House

Dedication

For everyone who's ever rebuilt their life with tea, toast, and a touch of magic.

You are braver than you know.

First published in Great Britain in 2025

by Beresford Publishing House,

Unit 34618, PO Box 4336, Manchester, M61 0BW

This edition first published in 2025

A CIP catalogue record for this book is available from the British Library.

ISBN: 978-1-913422-33-2

Cover illustration and design © PlainSight VFX.

Chapter 1

I STOOD ON THE doorstep watching the post van rattle down the drive in a cloud of dust, holding the envelope the postie had delivered like it might bite.

Since moving into Briarwood Gables several weeks back, I'd had a steady stream of official mail. Thick, textured documents were from Harlow and Fitch, my late grandmother's solicitors. They arrived with my name written in an artistic flourish on the front.

Then there were the ones from the accountant. Reams of paperwork trying to untangle the financial mess my husband had left behind. They came in thin white envelopes with the address labels printed in faint low-toner ink and slapped on at a crooked angle.

This letter was neither.

My name appeared in a spidery scrawl and an airmail label filled the top corner. The postmark read, Paraguay.

My fingers trembled so much I almost dropped it.

So, Paraguay really was a destination for husbands fleeing failed businesses and almost thirty years of marriage. Who knew?

I hesitated. Even if Gary had merely sent me a 'wish you were here' postcard, I wasn't sure I wanted to read it.

But what the heck? I ripped open the top and peeped inside.

'Notice of Divorce Proceedings' was typed in bold letters on the first page.

Wow. My husband really knew how to kick a girl when she was down. To think I'd ever trusted this man.

I dropped the papers into the envelope like they were radioactive waste.

"Bad timing, Gary," I muttered, tucking the envelope onto the hall table. I had no room in my head, or my heart, for selfish, disappearing, soon-to-be ex-husbands right now. Not on the morning I launched my new B&B, with my opening day guests arriving at any moment and a front door handle stuck like it had sworn to keep them out.

"Try it now," called Tom.

The handyman who my grandmother had let stay in the old caravan out the back was crouched by said door with a screwdriver in his hand.

He looked from me to the envelope with a slight frown. "You OK, Josie?" he asked. "Not bad news, I hope?"

I forced a smile. "I'm fine. Just pre-opening jitters." I turned my back on Gary's envelope and tried the door handle.

"Tom, you are a genius," I said, sighing with relief as the door opened smoothly. "You've saved my first visitors from having to climb in through the window."

Tom wiped his hands on his jeans and grinned. "Oh, I think a jammed door might be the least of your guests' problems," he said. "Honestly, Josie, I don't know what you were thinking about booking in two rival dance troupes. There's going to be a commotion once the Green Stags realise they're staying in the same place as the Crimson Bells."

I frowned. This wasn't the first time Tom had voiced his concerns about the teams of dancers due to check in at Briarwood Gables.

"You really think they're going to make trouble?" I asked. "It's a Morris Dancing Festival, not gang warfare."

Morris dancing, for the uninitiated (which included me until three weeks ago), is traditional, English folk dancing involving jingling bells, flying handkerchiefs, and the enthusiastic clashing of large wooden sticks. Think a whirlwind of choreographed combat in colourful costumes set to toe-tapping tunes. It's quaint, historic and, apparently, a powder keg of competitiveness.

Tom screwed his face up in a way that didn't fill me with confidence. "In the Briarvale contest, either the Stags win, or the Bells win. The rivalry is fierce."

"Well, they'll have to behave," I said. "I've worked too hard to get this place ready for everything to fall apart over a dance-off."

And it was true. I needed this to work.

Most of the small inheritance my grandmother had left me was already spent, poured into polishing every corner of this house and coaxing it into life. But Briarwood Gables was gleaming. Every spider had been gently relocated, every cobweb banished. The windows were polished, the old oak floors buffed to a warm, honeyed shine. Each guest room had its own colour scheme complete with cutesy floral wallpaper and antique furniture. Even the dining room was ready, set out with my best collection of mismatched chairs and tables, each of the latter with a tiny vase holding a spray of flowers I'd picked from the garden.

It had taken blood, sweat and more elbow grease than I thought possible, and I couldn't have done it without Tom's help. Especially as Einstein had not allowed one flicker of magic.

"Cleaning is character building," he'd said, while reclined on a stack of decorator's dust sheets like a furry, grey, supervising Roman emperor.

Einstein, for those new to this story, is my cat. Or, more precisely, my familiar. Now that I've turned fifty and officially come into my magical witch powers, I can understand everything he says. And believe me, Einstein has a lot to say.

My phone pinged, and a message from my daughter Kim appeared.

'Good luck with the grand opening today, Mum.'

Another message followed immediately with a photo of her six-year-old twins holding up a sign that read 'Good Luck Nana' in wobbly crayon letters. Both girls beamed at the camera.

I sent them three heart emojis, swallowing the usual ache that came when I remembered my daughter and grandchildren lived in Boston, an ocean away.

Right then, Einstein trotted down the staircase: a cat on a mission. At the same time, Murphy, Tom's collie, gave a short, sharp bark.

Einstein glared at him. "What I was coming to tell you before the mutt butted in," he said, "is that people are arriving."

Murphy barked again.

"But I saw them first," huffed Einstein.

I smoothed down my hair and took a deep breath, trying to swallow the rising wave of awkward menopausal heat that had inconveniently showed up at that moment.

"Right then," I said. "Show time."

I cast a last glance at the envelope on the table. The B&B had to work, if only to prove to Gary 'the Betrayer' Appleton that I was better off without him. Then I plastered on my best smile and opened the door.

A minibus with 'The Green Stags Morris Troupe' painted on the side had pulled up, and a group of folks all wearing matching green shirts tumbled out. As the self-appointed head of my welcoming committee, Murphy shot out of the door to greet them, his tail wagging enthusiastically.

I followed with a little more trepidation, glad that Tom was right behind me.

"Josie Appleton?" said the man who had been first out of the van. He looked around my age with grey hair and beard.

"That's right," I called.

"Geoff Mercer. We spoke on the phone." He offered a calloused hand that practically radiated good cheer. "Thanks again for letting us check in early, love. It'll be good to be settled before this afternoon's showdown."

"I'm happy to help," I beamed.

"Lovely spot you have here," said a woman coming up behind him. "I'm June, Geoff's wife. I'm the keeper of the dance costumes."

I'd expected all the dancers to be young, but apart from two women in their mid-twenties, the rest of the group were over forty and full of cheery banter. I handed out keys as they gathered in the hallway.

"Geoff and June, you've got the Rose Room," I said. "Maddie and Tasha, you're in six. Room four for the Hancocks, and Mr King is in room five."

"Hey, Daryl," shouted Geoff. "Come and get your key."

The last of the group was still standing outside, deep in conversation.

"Sorry, sorry," he said, ending the call. "Business. You know how it is."

He was tanned, tall and with the sort of grin that probably got him free drinks in bars. The air around him shimmered with enough aftershave to stun any small woodland creature within twenty metres, and Einstein gave a loud sneeze.

Geoff clapped his team-mate round the shoulders. "This is Daryl, our fearless leader. Keeps us all in line. Mostly."

"He's the brains behind all the fancy footwork that's going to win the contest today," June told me.

"Oh, we'll definitely be keeping our title," Daryl said with a confident grin. "Our new routine is going to knock your socks off."

"Would you mind if we have a last run through on your lawn before we head out?" Geoff asked as I led the group up the stairs.

"Of course you can," I said. "I'd love a sneak preview."

To my relief, everyone offered compliments about their rooms, so I left them to settle in.

"So far, so good," I said to Tom as I returned to the hallway.

Tom smiled. "You've done a fantastic job with the house, Josie. You should be proud."

I blushed at his praise. "I wouldn't have managed half of it without your help."

Einstein, who had been sitting on the stairs keeping a watchful eye on the proceedings, gave a loud, exaggerated yawn. "Yes, yes," he said. "You've both done a stellar job. Truly heart-warming. I'll knit you both a medal, shall I?"

I scowled at him, and he started the rumbling, purring laugh he does when he's amused himself.

But the Green Stags were coming downstairs again. They began unloading sticks and bells from the back of the van. However, before they could so much as jingle a leg, a convoy of cars rolled up the drive.

Three of them.

And from the way the members of the Green Stags froze at the sight of them, I didn't even need to look at the name stuck to their sun visors.

The Crimson Bells had arrived.

Chapter 2

T HE GREEN STAGS STOOD immobile as the three cars belonging to the Crimson Bells did an impressive display of synchronised parking, slotting themselves in a perfect arc around the Stags' minibus.

Tom, watching from the porch with Murphy at his feet, gave a low whistle. "Here comes trouble."

"Well, this should be interesting," muttered Einstein. He jumped onto the porch rail and gave a slow, ominous flick of his tail. "Maybe you should have baked some Serenity Scones."

I gulped. As well as turning the house into a functioning B&B, I'd spent many hours practising my magical baking from recipes from ancient cookbooks left to me by my witchy ancestors in Briarwood Gables' secret library. Serenity Scones were one of my best recipes, and right now, they were possibly my most needed. Why hadn't I thought to make them sooner?

The first car door swung open and a tall, sharp-looking man in a crimson polo shirt stepped out, aviator sunglasses gleaming like he was the star of *Top Gun: Folk Dancing Edition.* He turned a lazily amused gaze on the Green Stags and grinned.

"Well, well," he said. "Didn't realise we were checking into enemy territory." He nodded at the sticks the Stags were holding. "Looks like we arrived just in time. Don't let us stop you practising. You'll need every second, if you're going to beat us this year."

"Well, you're too late, Liam," Daryl retorted, collecting the sticks he'd just handed out and stowing them swiftly back into the van. "Practice time is over."

I groaned. What if the Green Stags lost because they didn't have their last rehearsal? Would they blame me for booking their rivals in?

"Come on, Daryl," Liam was saying. "Show us what your A-game looks like." He gave a lazy grin as he removed his sunglasses. "Hope your bribes are as impressive as last year's, or you might actually have to earn your win by dancing."

There was a sharp intake of breath from the Green Stags, and June muttered something under her breath that sounded suspiciously like, "Here we go again." Daryl, however, stayed surprisingly calm and cool. He gave Liam a confident smile and turned away. June let out an audible sigh of relief.

The rest of the Crimson Bells were piling out of their cars. Apart from one older couple, most looked to be in their thirties. They were fit, cheerful, and smug in a way that suggested they were used to winning.

Geoff from the Stags approached the older man from the Bells with a warm smile. "Hey, Rupert," he said. "I thought you lot were staying at The Briar and Thorn?"

"They had a burst pipe, so we had to change at the last minute," Rupert told him. He glanced at Briarwood Gables. "But this place looks OK."

"Wait till you see the rooms," put in June enthusiastically, coming up behind her husband. "They're lovely."

Encouraged that we'd avoided stick fights at dawn, I crunched across the gravel towards the dancers with my best B&B-owner smile.

"Hi, there," I said, louder than was probably necessary. "I'm Josie. Great to meet the Crimson Bells. Let's get you all inside and settled, shall we?"

There was a general shuffle of luggage and mildly competitive muttering as the Bells followed me into the house, while Tom told the Stags about the river that ran along the boundary of the property and the menagerie of animals they would find there.

"Well, that wasn't so bad," I whispered to him as we passed on the drive. "Just friendly banter."

Tom raised an eyebrow. "Wait until one of them loses."

Half an hour later, Briarwood Gables was officially full of its first paying guests. The earlier tension between the Stags and the Bells seemed to be forgotten, and Murphy had earned his title as my best ice-breaking employee.

I watched as the dance troupes loaded into their cars. The Crimson Bells left first, eagerly chatting about eating pastries from Briarvale's tearoom, The HoneyPot, run by my good friend Sylvia. The Green Stags followed with a more serious conversation about the timing of steps and formations.

Tom also headed to his pickup. "Want a lift to the village?"

I hesitated.

"You *are* going to the festival, aren't you?" he asked.

"Well, I thought I should stay here," I told him. "I'm a land-lady now. What if any of the guests want to come back?"

"You've given them their keys," Tom reasoned.

"Well, yes..."

"There's the dancing competition itself in the afternoon and the post-competition party this evening," he wheedled. "You're not seriously going to miss all that, are you?"

Einstein brushed past my legs as he headed through the door. "Oh, we have to go," he said. "I've watched the event with every witch since it started."

Tom opened the door to the pickup and Murphy bounded onto the seat. "You coming, or not?"

"Let me grab a cardigan," I decided, dashing inside.

But as I scooted through the hallway, I caught sight of something that made me stop dead.

Despite it being barely midday, the hands on the grandfather clock pointed to twenty past four.

A chill ran down my spine.

In the short time I'd lived at Briarwood Gables, I'd learned that the old clock never told the actual time, rather it had a knack for predicting events. Some, like my arrival at the house, had been good. Others had been more ominous. There was the man murdered near my greenhouse, and my getting shot at by his killer.

"Oh, brilliant," I muttered, as I fetched my cardigan from the kitchen. "Because what this day really needs is a dash of unexpected something."

Whatever it was, I hoped it wouldn't spell trouble for my B&B.

Tom was waiting in his pickup, and I pushed the worry about what might happen at 4.20 pm out of my mind as we rumbled down the winding country lane to Briarvale.

It was a perfect day. Golden sunlight spilled over rolling green hills and wildflowers swayed lazily in the warm June breeze. Hedgerows burst with colour, framing the road like an artist's watercolour, and overhead swallows darted through the sky, letting out short, excited calls.

My anticipation mounted as we neared the village, and as we crossed the humpback bridge over Briar Brook, the scene before me didn't disappoint. Briarvale had blossomed into a riot of colour and excitement. The green was awash with stalls showcasing everything from knitted tea cosies to handmade chocolates and jars of dubious chutney, their owners beaming with the pride of people who've found an audience for their particular passions.

Gaily coloured bunting fluttered between the stalls, and brightly dressed dancers from all over the country filled every nook and cranny. Tom found a parking spot on the far side of the green, and I wandered through the chaos, mesmerised.

"I had no idea Morris dancing was such a big deal," I remarked to Tom, dodging a group of men with tiny bells fastened round their knees.

Dance troupes held impromptu practice sessions wherever they found a space, and the rhythmic clacking of sticks mingled with laughter and good-natured ribbing.

"You call that a caper? My gran can leap higher, and she's had both hips replaced!" one dancer teased another.

I laughed.

"Fancy a pastry from The Honeypot?" I asked Tom. "I owe you big time for all the help you've given me with the house."

Tom grinned. "It's been my pleasure," he said, "but I never say no to some of Sylvia's home cooking."

As we wended our way across the green, I was surprised to see the Crimson Bells in action outside the tearoom, a flurry of sticks, stomping boots and boundless energy.

Extra tables had been set out on the pavement outside, expanding Briarvale's beloved tea-room into an impromptu festival hub. Sylvia herself was taking orders like she was commanding an army of hungry villagers. She had a smudge of flour on her cheek, a streak of tomato ketchup on her apron, and the beaming smile of everyone's favourite auntie.

As soon as she spotted me, her dark curls bounced with delight, and she waved us over.

"Josie, love! And Tom!" she beamed. "How's Briarwood Gables holding up? The Bells were full of praise for the rooms."

"That's a relief," I said, with a touch of pride. "There's only breakfast to navigate in the morning, but I feel more confident with Paula to help me. Thanks for introducing us, by the way. You saved my life with that one. I was dreading having to cook breakfast for so many people on my own.

"No worries," chuckled Sylvia. "Paula needed some extra cash for her holidays, so it's a good deal for both of you."

I glanced toward the Bells, their routine a glorious mix of precision and barely controlled chaos.

"Looks like you're getting a full show from them," I said, marvelling at their energy and commitment to the craft of stick-wielding enthusiasm.

Sylvia smiled fondly.

"Oh, this has become rather a tradition," she explained. "The lads have been dancing outside The HoneyPot since they were young. Lovely folks."

She watched them with pure enjoyment.

"I used to give them free pastries."

Her face dimpled with pleasure.

"I still do."

Sudden raised voices from the far table interrupted our chat. I recognised the voice even before I'd turned round. It was Eva Henshaw, chair of the Parish Council, mastermind of every village event, self-appointed guardian of Briarvale's traditions, and all-round busybody. Her grey hair was styled with its usual military precision, and she wore her formal village event attire: a tweed skirt, sensible shoes, and a hand-knitted cardigan, despite the warmth of the day.

Eva had been rather frosty towards me when I first moved to Briarvale. I tried not to take it personally. I don't think she liked any newcomer to the village, full stop. But since I gifted her the Wedgwood tea service I'd received as a fiftieth birthday present before I moved from London, she'd grudgingly tolerated me.

Today, however, she wasn't tolerating anyone. Her face was flushed with anger as she squared up to a portly man wearing a judge's sash.

"If you think for one moment that you can bully me, Ronald Burrows, you've got another think coming!" Eva's voice cut through the cheerful chatter. "My organisation of this contest is exemplary, as always. And if you say otherwise, I'll see to it personally that you never judge another competition!"

With that, Eva stomped off, leaving stunned silence in her wake.

Ronald lingered long enough to flick a glance at the Crimson Bells as he passed.

"Still dancing for your dinner like you were a kid, Cardew?" he sneered. "Guess some things never change."

Ronald's voice wasn't loud, but by the scowl on Liam Cardew's face, he heard every word.

"Oh dear," Sylvia sighed, shaking her head. She leaned in close, her voice dropping to a conspiratorial whisper as Ronald Burrows walked off in the direction of the main arena. "That man is one of the judges and he's not exactly Mr Popularity around here."

"That's putting it mildly," commented Tom.

"Ronald can be rather harsh with his words," Sylvia explained. "He judges the annual flower show too, and I thought

Eva was going to throttle him with her hanging basket when it only took second prize last year."

"He must have a death wish if he was criticising Eva's organisational skills," Tom added. "Eva runs these events like clockwork."

I shook my head in disbelief. Who'd have believed this quaint little village was so surprisingly cut-throat?

And if Eva Henshaw was anything to go by, it wasn't only the dancers whose tempers were running high.

Chapter 3

C LUTCHING A FEAST OF cheese and tomato sandwiches and slices of fruitcake, we left Sylvia to tend to her many customers.

"We should find a place by the arena," Tom advised, leading me through the crowds, "before it gets too crowded and all the good spots are gone."

A section in the middle of the green had been roped off to form the competition arena, and there was a makeshift stage constructed from a farm trailer at one end. Someone had draped it in sheets and festooned it with garlands of flowers, giving it a cheerful, summery, festive feel. On the top were three chairs and a trestle table, neatly arranged for the judges.

Eva was already up there, fussing over name cards, notepads, pencils, water bottles, and results envelopes, all of which she was aligning with the precision of a woman convinced that chaos could be fought with stationery.

Her progress, however, was hindered by the dog leash in her hand. Charlie, her Shorkie (a cross between a Shih Tzu and a Yorkshire Terrier with the face of a teddy bear and the temperament of a chaos demon), had other plans. With the skill of a professional trip hazard, he lassoed his lead around one of the judge's chairs, then darted off to investigate something tantalisingly sniff-worthy at the back of the trailer, dragging the chair with him in a scraping clatter.

"Charlie!" Eva's voice rose to an exasperated screech.

As the chair juddered off the platform and thumped onto the grass, Charlie gave a delighted yip and tugged harder. Eva, struggling to keep hold of the lead while trying to maintain her dignity and her balance, let go with a huff of frustration. Charlie, thrilled at the sudden opportunity to explore the super-exciting smells that the wheels of the farm trailer had brought with them, made a break for it.

Luckily, Daryl from the Green Stags was standing by the stage. With the lightning reflexes of someone used to precision footwork, he stomped lightly on the lead as Charlie paused to sniff something sheep-related and then bent to scoop up the little dog with both hands.

"Gotcha, you little menace," he said cheerfully, holding Charlie out like a disgruntled prize. He hopped easily onto the stage with the dog squirming gently in his arms.

"Thank you, Daryl," Eva said, straightening up and brushing off her skirt. "Charlie's been impossible today."

"No trouble at all," Daryl replied. "He only wanted a front-row seat." He passed Charlie back to Eva with a warm grin, then he leaned a hip against the table with the casual ease of a man comfortable in the limelight.

"So, this is where our fates are sealed, eh?" he said, tapping one of the envelopes lightly with a fingertip. "I always imagine judges take one look at us and toss a coin."

Eva rolled her eyes. "I can assure you, there's a bit more to it than that."

Daryl laughed, brushing Shorkie hair from his waistcoat. "Well, I'll let you get back to commanding the battlefield," he said, as he hopped lightly off the stage.

Eva, with Charlie tucked safely into the crook of her arm, bent down to reposition the chair he had upended. Then she returned to straightening a name card and a rogue bottle of water that had somehow edged out of line.

Tom and I sat on the grass in companionable silence, unwrapping our sandwiches and watching the fun as we ate. He looked smart today. Not in a slick, polished way, but in a gentle, quietly capable sort of way; a man who could fix a broken gate and remember how I take my coffee. I honestly didn't know how I'd have got the B&B ready without him. From scrubbing years of soot out of the fireplace to wrestling the ancient plumbing into submission, he'd quietly got on with it. No fuss. No drama. Just Tom.

He caught me looking. "What? Have I got mayo on my face?"

I smiled and shook my head. "No. I was thinking how glad I am that you didn't run for the hills after day three of rewiring the boiler in Briarwood Gables."

Tom gave a mock shudder. "Ah, the boiler rewire. Dark days."

We both laughed. Murphy flopped beside us, tongue lolling in the heat, while Einstein curled himself round my feet. On one side of the arena there was a fiddle tuning up, on the other a piper playing a lively jig, and the ever-present jingle of the bells strapped to the dancers' legs sounded from all directions.

It all felt... perfect.

Ten minutes later, the judges climbed onto the stage.

There were three of them. Ronald Burrows, the man Eva had argued with earlier, looking as surly and disagreeable as before. Next to him sat Reverend Peters from Briarvale church. The third man I didn't recognise. He was mid-fifties, and he obviously took pride in his appearance. From his navy, tailored blazer and the shine on his expensive shoes, to the clever cut of his greying hair which minimised the balding patch on the top of his head, he reminded me of my soon-to-be ex-husband, which wasn't a good omen.

"I bet people don't like that other judge either," I commented, thinking of Gary.

"Too right," Tom agreed. "That's Marcus Langley. He's a hot shot lawyer from London. He bought a massive mansion by the sea at Polvarren as a second home and his la-di-dah wife holds exclusive parties there. No-one likes that." He took another bite of his sandwich and chewed thoughtfully. "Marcus doesn't get involved with us 'locals' apart from this dance competition, which it appears he's somewhat of an expert on."

Tom might have said more, but Eva's sharp voice suddenly blared through the PA system and cut him off.

"Ladies and gentlemen, esteemed visitors and spirited dancers, welcome to this year's Briarvale South-West Regional Morris Dancing Festival."

She was still cradling Charlie as though he were the world's fluffiest baby.

"Good luck to you all, and may the best team win!"

The crowd erupted in cheers and applause, and I found myself clapping along, caught up in the enthusiasm.

I glanced around, wondering where Percy, her long-suffering husband, or Florence, her perpetually anxious Parish Council assistant, had got to. They were usually tasked with Charlie-minding when Eva was in official village business mode. I didn't have to wait long to find out.

Chapter 4

"**F**IRST UP," EVA ANNOUNCED, "is Briarvale's very own Whirligig Wobblers!"

"I didn't know we had our own team," I said, as the crowd whooped and cheered.

Tom let out a hearty laugh. "Oh, we do." He tapped the side of his nose. "The only year they ever got on the scoreboard was the year Ronald Burrows coached them. They came third. Then his wife died, and he took up judging instead."

"Well, it's the taking part that counts, right?" I offered diplomatically, as six familiar faces made their way to the centre of the arena.

There was Harold, the local librarian, looking scholarly and composed. Pippa, the flamboyant landlady from The Briar and Thorn, beaming at the crowd. Percy, Eva's neat-freak husband, scanning the crowd like he was filing a risk assessment, and poor nervous Florence, Eva's usual shadow, who seemed ready to bolt at any moment. Edwin from the grocery store cheerily waved a large orange handkerchief at the crowd, and Dr Hale... well, Dr Hale looked like he'd rather be anywhere else.

"Oh, this should be good," Tom muttered beside me.

The Briarvale Primary School string ensemble struck up a jaunty tune, and the Whirligig Wobblers launched into their routine.

Within the first ten seconds, Harold and Edwin collided mid-twirl, their sticks clattering to the ground.

"Is that supposed to happen?" I whispered to Tom.

He stifled a laugh. "Not exactly, but it's all part of the charm, eh?"

I watched with a mix of horror and delight as the performance unfolded. Florence, her face set in grim determination, was whacking her sticks with Pippa like she was fighting off a home invasion. Dr Hale, meanwhile, seemed to be dancing to an entirely different tune, his movements reminiscent of a robot attempting the Charleston.

"They're certainly... enthusiastic," I managed, trying to keep a straight face as Pippa narrowly avoided Percy's wildly swinging arm.

Tom chuckled. "That's one word for it."

"I hope there's an ambulance on standby," I laughed.

As the dance reached its crescendo, with sticks flying and dancers skipping and stumbling, I found myself swept up in the sheer joy of it all.

When the final notes faded and the Whirligig Wobblers took their bows (miraculously avoiding further collisions), I joined in the thunderous applause.

"Well," I said, wiping tears of laughter from my eyes, "I think I finally understand the appeal of Morris dancing."

Although I noticed Ronald Burrows was shaking his head like he'd witnessed a particularly troubling routine choreographed by a group of overenthusiastic octopi.

Eva cleared her throat with the sort of authority that suggested decades of experience and zero tolerance for faff.

"The next team," she announced, "is the Black Boars from Upper Trevenna."

From the corner of the arena emerged three men and three women dressed in black waistcoats adorned with ribbons, white shirts, and black trousers with bells strapped to their knees. Each of them carried a stick about two feet long, polished to a shine that caught the afternoon sun.

"They look rather fierce," I commented to Tom, as the team took their positions in a precise formation.

"They're known for their aggressive style," he replied. "Watch how they clash those sticks. They've broken a fair few fingers over the years."

I shuddered.

Thankfully, there were no injuries this time.

More teams followed. The Red Rovers performed acrobatic leaps that drew gasps from the crowd. The Yellow Jackets executed such rapid legwork that the sound of their bells was a constant, shimmering jingle. And the Springfield Ramblers from the nearby town of Polvarren incorporated juggling into their dance routing, tossing their sticks between themselves with breath-taking confidence.

Murphy, bored with the whole affair, went to sleep on the grass. Einstein was feigning indifference, but I caught the occasional twitch of his tail as though he was secretly assessing every detail of the competition.

Then it was the turn of the Crimson Bells.

Liam and the others marched into the arena with Rambo-style war-paint on their faces like Morris dancing had suddenly become a contact sport. The Bells moved with surprising grace for a group of such varied ages and builds, their feet executing intricate steps while their upper bodies remained almost rigidly controlled. When they brought their sticks together in a series of rhythmic clashes, the sound was sharp and precise.

"They're good," Einstein remarked. "That performance might be enough to win them the title this year."

"Do you think *I* should take up Morris dancing?" I mused. "I've been doing everything else since I moved here. It might help shift my middle-age spread."

Tom gave me a sideways smile. "You've changed plenty already, Josie. Some of us are still catching up."

Did he mean the house, the village, or something entirely different? But Tom had gone back to watching the dancers again, his expression unreadable.

A breeze picked up as the Crimson Bells left the arena, tugging at loose strands of my hair and bringing with it the mingled scents of grass and frying onions from the burger stall.

Eva strode onto the stage carrying her clipboard with the determination of a general heading into battle. "Thank you, the Crimson Bells," she said into the microphone.

But an unexpected gust of warm summer wind swept across the village green. It caught the envelopes on the judges' table, scattering them over the stage like oversized confetti.

Eva, with the efficiency of someone who had weathered far worse crises, bent to retrieve them, her knees cracking in protest. She gathered the wayward envelopes, then replaced them back on the table, one in front of each judge, and the competition carried on.

There was an all-girl troupe called the Merry Maids, followed by the lively Dancing Hares, whose set ended up with one member tripping over a dropped stick and falling flat on their face.

"And now," Eva announced, her voice carrying a hint of extra formality, "the final team. The champions of last year's competition. The Green Stags."

A hush fell over the crowd as the Stags stepped into the area. They were dressed in forest green waistcoats and crisp white trousers. Unlike the other teams, who'd entered with good-natured waves and cheeky grins, the Green Stags moved with a focus that bordered on intensity.

Within moments, it was clear why they were the reigning champions. Their movements were impossibly synchronised. Their sticks met in the air with precision, creating distinct, rhythmic patterns, and when they launched into a series of high jumps, it was as if gravity had temporarily suspended itself for them.

I hardly dared to breathe for fear something might go wrong. Even Einstein abandoned his pretence of indifference, his amber eyes tracking the dancers with undisguised interest.

When they finished, the crowd erupted into wild applause. The Green Stags exited the arena with practiced bows. Ronald Burrows, however, still wore the same unimpressed scowl.

I glanced at my watch: 4:17 PM. It looked as though the grandfather clock at Briarwood Gables was pointing to the time the competition results would be announced. I could live with that.

The final dance had barely finished when Eva strode to the centre of the green, raising a polished wooden box aloft as if she was about to auction it off.

"Now comes the theatrical part," Tom told me. "Eva loves to drag out announcing the winners."

"Ladies and gentlemen!" Eva's voice rang across the crowd, crackling slightly through the PA system. "The judges will now record their decisions."

She approached the judges' table with exaggerated ceremony and set the box down with a flourish. "Please write the names of your top three teams on the score card beside you," she instructed. "Seal it in the envelope provided, then deposit it in the box. No peeking, no conferring, and absolutely no take-backs."

The judges took up their pens. Reverend Peters scribbled away with enthusiasm, Marcus Langley frowned as if solving a particularly difficult crossword puzzle, and Ronald Burrows moved with painstaking deliberation, his pen gliding slowly across the paper, lips pursed as if he were finalising the closing arguments before the Supreme Court.

When the last envelope had been sealed and safely tucked inside the box, Eva collected it with the care of someone handling antique crystal.

"And now," she said, "to tally the votes."

A ripple of anticipation passed through the crowd.

With deliberate slowness, Eva opened the lid and began removing the envelopes. One by one, she tore them open.

The opening scorecard placed the Crimson Bells in the lead ahead of the Green Stags and the Black Boars. A triumphant chorus rose from the corner of the green where a group of crimson shirts were already celebrating like they'd won the lottery.

The following set of marks flipped the result: Green Stags first, Bells second, Red Rovers third. This time, a delighted roar surged from the Stags' camp, with fists pumping and a few dance moves that probably weren't regulation.

With the Stags and the Bells now neck and neck, all eyes turned to Eva and the final ranking. The crowd held its collective breath, the silence broken only by the persistent breeze rustling through the bunting decorating the stage.

Slowly, reverently, Eva drew out the last envelope. Her expression revealing nothing as she slid out the score card it contained.

"Claiming the third spot," she told the waiting competitors, "are the Red Rovers."

There was a polite round of applause.

Eva surveyed the impatient crowd as though she were announcing a royal decree. "Second position goes to the Black Boars."

An expectant hush fell over the village green.

Eva held the moment.

"But in first place," she announced crisply, "are the Green Stags. Long may their bells jingle."

The crowd broke into applause, punctuated by cheers and the odd disappointed groan.

Eva smiled broadly. "Which means the winners of this year's Briarvale South-West Regional Morris Dancing Festival..." she paused for absolute maximum effect, "...are the Green Stags!"

I let out a sigh of relief. At least missing their final rehearsal because I'd booked them into Briarwood Gables with the Bells hadn't cost the Stags the trophy.

Geoff and June shared a celebratory kiss while Daryl and the others whooped triumphantly and pumped their fists in celebration.

In contrast, Liam from the Crimson Bells stormed past us, his expression as fierce as the war paint still streaked across his face. He was muttering something about 'didn't even get a vote from the third judge' and 'I bet that was Burrows'.

But our attention was drawn to the stage. Ronald Burrows had risen from his chair, one hand clutched to his chest, the other braced against the table. His face had turned an alarming shade of red, his eyes bulging behind his spectacles.

At first, I thought he was simply overcome by the result. But then he crumpled to the ground with a thud.

Marcus Langley jumped to his feet, pushing back his chair so violently that it toppled over, and Reverend Peters fell to his knees beside Ronald, already shouting for help.

I checked my watch again: exactly 4:20 PM.

An icy feeling settled in my stomach as I realised that *this* was the event the grandfather clock had been referring to.

Chapter 5

RONALD BURROWS LAY UNNATURALLY still on the stage.

The cheers of the crowd had given way to confused murmurs as the seriousness of what had happened began to sink in.

Eva stood frozen at the microphone, the prize-giving ceremony she'd been about to lead forgotten as she stared at the motionless figure before her.

"Is he having a heart attack?" someone nearby asked.

"Where's Dr Hale?" asked another, more urgently.

Calls for the doctor echoed across Briarvale Green, and after what seemed like an eternity, but must only have been seconds, the crowd parted and Dr Hale emerged at a run, still wearing his Whirligig Wobblers costume, the bells jingling as he raced towards the judges' table.

Einstein hopped onto my knee. "It's 4.20, isn't it?" he purred. "The grandfather clock is never wrong. I'm going for a closer look."

And before I could stop him, he disappeared behind the stage, slipping through the confusion like a shadow.

Dr Hale knelt beside Ronald Burrows, pressing two fingers against the man's neck. His expression remained neutral, but something about the set of his shoulders told me everything. It wasn't good.

Next minute, he pulled out his mobile, his voice carrying across the hush that had fallen over the green.

"This is Dr Vincent Hale. Ambulance required at Briarvale village green immediately. Male, sixty-five, possible cardiac arrest."

The words rippled through the crowd like an Artic wind.

Reverend Peters stood at the judging table, his usually beaming face drawn and solemn as he bowed his head, his lips moving in a silent prayer.

Eva fired into action. "Give him air," she commanded, her voice steady even though the shock was clearly etched on her face.

Florence stepped away from the Whirlygig Wobblers and dashed towards the stage. For once, she wasn't trembling in Eva's shadow but was surprisingly firm as she directed people away from the stage.

"I'll give them a hand," said Tom, already striding forward to help.

Behind me, I caught snatches of conversation from a knot of the Springfield Ramblers.

"Well, that's the way to put a dampener on the day," one muttered, adjusting the bells on his calf.

"Hardly his fault," another replied, though without much conviction.

"Pity it didn't happen before he gave his verdict," a third added with a grim chuckle. "Ron always marks us down."

A chill passed through me that had nothing to do with the summer breeze. The callousness of their remarks was shocking but revealing. Ronald Burrows clearly hadn't been popular with anybody... and now he was dead.

I glanced at Eva, who was still maintaining order with remarkable composure, though her face had lost some of its colour. For a woman often referred to as Briarvale's self-appointed dictator, she suddenly looked small.

On the stage, Einstein was winding his way between the chairs. Anyone else might've seen a local moggy doing the rounds, but I knew he was a cat on a mission.

Charlie had spotted him, too. The tiny dog yapped and bounced furiously on the end of his lead, ears flat, his whole body wired with frustration as Percy held him from getting to his arch-enemy.

Einstein, meanwhile, was conducting a full forensic sweep. He pressed a paw to the table as if testing for vibrations, sniffed the results box discarded by the mic stand, and brushed past Reverend Peters, who froze mid-prayer and searched the crowd until he located me.

He pointed at Einstein and raised an eyebrow.

Time to retrieve my feline accomplice.

I sighed and deliberately took my time climbing onto the stage, giving Einstein as much opportunity as possible to complete his inspection.

"Einstein, for heaven's sake," I chided him, adding a sigh to complete the act.

Trying not to look at the group gathered round Ronald, I reached to scoop him up, steadying myself against the judges' table as I did so.

The wood was warm. Too warm.

And suddenly, the world tilted.

The crowd shimmered. Time itself seemed to shift. And for a brief, impossible moment, I felt something.

Longing. A deep, aching affection that didn't belong to me. A presence. A heartache so fierce it stopped me dead.

My vision swam, and in the centre of the haze, I was looking at a woman in the crowd. Chestnut hair. Beautiful. Calculated. Watching.

Then she was gone.

"Josie?" Einstein's voice cut through the fog. He stared at me, his investigation abandoned.

"Oh boy," I breathed.

That was another vision.

Just like before.

Psychometry, Einstein had called it. The ability to read the energy imprints left on an object by touching it. It's pretty advanced witch stuff, and the strain had knocked me unconscious last time.

I gasped and sat down hard on Marcus Langley's chair, taking deep breaths. I didn't want to hit the deck with the whole village watching.

Einstein jumped onto my lap, purring louder than an express train and pressing himself against me. "Did you get something?" he asked.

I nodded, running my fingers through his silky, grey fur, letting the comforting warmth from his body calm me. Slowly, the light-headed feeling began to recede.

"At least you didn't pass out this time," Einstein noted with the faintest purr of satisfaction at my progress.

Still clutching him to me, I stood up and tottered to the edge of the stage.

"Josie!"

Tom was at the steps to the stage, concern etched across his features.

"You've gone white," he said. His gaze flicked toward where Ronald Burrows lay on the floor. "Is it because of..."

"I'm... fine," I stuttered.

Tom held out his hand. "Come on, let's get you off there. There's nothing we can do."

I blinked hard, clearing the lingering fog of the vision. "I... I'm fine," I repeated, but all the same, I was glad of his steady arm as I climbed down from the trailer.

We walked a short way from the stage and sat on the grass. The crowd was already beginning to disperse. People drifted toward the market stalls, speaking in hushed tones about what they'd witnessed. I noticed that few of them spared more than a passing glance for the fallen judge.

"Dr Hale's still trying, but it doesn't look good," Tom said quietly. "The ambulance is on its way, but..." He didn't finish the sentence. He didn't need to.

Einstein climbed off my lap and sat directly in front of me. His posture was unusually straight, his tail curved neatly around his paws. He fixed me with a steady gaze, his eyes practically glowing with certainty.

"Ronald Burrows did not die from a dodgy heart," he declared with the confidence of a pathologist delivering his findings. "He was poisoned with cyanide."

"What?" I blurted, forgetting momentarily that, to everyone else, Einstein was just a cat making typical cat noises.

"Aww, don't shout at him," said Tom, misinterpreting my outburst completely. He bent down and scooped Einstein into his arms. "He probably wants some food," he said, scratching behind Einstein's ears in a way that would normally have earned him a swift swat from a well-aimed claw.

However, for once Einstein tolerated the handling with unusual grace. "I could smell bitter almonds," he mewed, looking directly at me over Tom's shoulder. "Trust me, Ronald Burrows has been poisoned. Oh, and now you mention it, I *am* hungry. Starving, in fact. Sleuthing gives me an appetite."

"Poison," I blurted out without thinking, ignoring Einstein's culinary requests.

My mind raced.

Had someone right here at the festival poisoned Ronald Burrows?

"Poison?" Tom echoed, his brow furrowing.

I scrambled for an explanation that wouldn't make me sound like I was conversing with my cat. "Not 'poison'," I said, improvising wildly. "I was telling Einstein to... keep his 'paws in'. He's always swiping at things."

Tom's puzzled expression deepened, but Einstein began batting at the air as if chasing an invisible butterfly, a performance so uncharacteristic of his usual dignified demeanour that I nearly laughed, in spite of the gravity of the situation.

"Well, you're a strange one, aren't you?" Tom said, half to me, half to the cat. Then he gently lowered Einstein back on the ground.

"You owe me big time for this," Einstein spat grumpily, shaking out his whiskers.

I bent down beside him. "You got 'poison' from a smell?" I whispered.

"Cyanide has a rather distinctive aroma. It was on the envelopes in the results box," he told me.

"And you recognise the scent of cyanide?" I said, not sure whether I should be worried about that.

"It can be incorporated into some spells. Some of the Stanton witches used it, but Beatrix didn't like to," Einstein said matter-of-factly. "I don't think we have any."

"Well, I'm glad about that," I breathed.

"Anyway, there were two really potent scents in the box, and one was definitely cyanide," Einstein finished with a firm nod of his head, like a feline Hercules Poirot revealing a crucial but inconclusive clue.

"What was the other one?" I asked.

"I don't know yet," he admitted. "But I've smelled it before. It's lodged in my brain like a stuck hairball. I'm sure it'll come to me."

Around us, the drama continued to evolve. Eva's face had turned paler than ever, and she leaned heavily on Florence's arm. Percy stood nearby. He'd picked Charlie up and tucked him under one arm whilst he scribbled notes into a small leather-bound book, his station master's meticulousness finding a new purpose in documenting the unfortunate event.

A few dancers lingered at the scene, looking rather subdued. The Green Stags, their victory celebration abruptly cut short, huddled near the stage, their expressions tinged with disappointment mingled with the uncomfortable awareness that their moment of triumph would be forever shadowed by the death of Ronald Burrows.

In the distance, came the rising wail of sirens.

Another murder in Briarvale!

The idea seemed completely at odds with the village's quaint charm and tight-knit community. And yet... the dancers' lack of sympathy, the argument in the tearoom, and the precise timing of Ronald's collapse all pointed in one direction.

Cyanide poisoning.

If Einstein was right, and in my experience he rarely wasn't, then Ronald's death hadn't been an accident. It had been calculated. Deliberate. And the killer was almost certainly still among us.

I scanned the crowd.

Were they still here, watching the aftermath of their handiwork, satisfaction neatly disguised as shock?

I shivered even in the warmth of the June sun.

Beside me, Einstein sat completely still, his eyes watching too, as if already assembling a suspect list.

The dancing may be over, but a far deadlier contest had only just begun.

Chapter 6

THE AMBULANCE TORE INTO the village square in a blaze of sirens that cut through the afternoon calm. Flickering blue lights strobed over the crowd, warping Briarvale's chocolate-box charm into something strangely disjointed. Like reality had glitched and dropped Briarvale into a futuristic timeline.

Two paramedics leapt out and rushed toward the judges' table with a stretcher. Dr Hale looked relieved as he stepped back to let the ambulance crew take over, but his expression remained grim.

One paramedic knelt beside Ronald, checking for signs of life, while the other got some equipment ready. I couldn't hear what was being said, but I saw the brief pause, the sharp look exchanged between them, a flicker of something that suggested more than a standard medical emergency.

One of them glanced toward Dr Hale, then at the crowd, his brow furrowed together.

"Something's not right," I murmured to Tom.

Before he had time to reply, a familiar car rolled up and out stepped DI Holloway, moving like he owned the place, which, to be fair, he did once a crime was involved.

We'd crossed paths before, back when a body inconveniently appeared outside my greenhouse, and he hadn't exactly been thrilled that I'd cracked that case before he did.

His exact words had been, "Tell Mrs Appleton not to even think about starting a detective agency," which, in my opinion, was both rude and a shocking underestimation.

It also reminded me of my soon-to-be ex-husband.

The DI surveyed the square with that same hawk-eyed intensity I remembered all too well.

He spoke briefly with the paramedics, then with Dr Hale, before turning his gaze on the dispersing crowd like a raptor assessing its prey.

A second police car pulled in. Two more officers I remembered from the murder at Briarwood Gables hurried to the stage.

DI Holloway gestured towards the judges' table, and they quickly started stringing blue and white tape around the trailer.

"They're treating it as a crime scene," I said, the reality of Einstein's poison theory thickening like one of my doomed, lumpy, custard experiments in the kitchen.

Tom frowned. "It does look a bit dramatic for a natural death," he agreed.

"Exactly," I muttered. "And do you remember how DI Holloway handled things when we found Graham Prescott in the garden?"

Tom shuddered. "Don't remind me. I hope he's not going to arrest me again."

Einstein brushed against my ankles, his tail flicking smugly. "The ambulance guys must have noticed the almond smell too," he said, as casually as if announcing the weather.

My stomach dropped, and a wave of heat flushed up my neck.

For once, it wasn't the fifty-something hormonal kind, rather the oh-no-someone's-dead-again kind. Suddenly, my throat had gone dry.

"I'm going to buy a lemonade," I muttered.

With Einstein trotting by my side, I made a beeline for the refreshment stall.

Because when life gives you murder... you need lemonade, right?

As I waited in the queue, I spotted Sally Barnes weaving through the crowd, her brood of children trailing behind her like disorderly ducklings. Sally had been a good friend since I arrived in Briarvale. The youngest child, Benji, was enthusiastically smacking his sisters with a stick.

"I'm a Green Stag!" he shouted.

"Mum!" Millie, his sister, wailed. "He's hitting me!"

Sally let out a world-weary sigh.

"Benji, if you touch anyone else with that stick, I swear I will make you eat it."

Her face brightened as she caught sight of me. Adjusting her course, she navigated through the throng with the practiced ease of a woman who had spent years manoeuvring a small army of children through crowded spaces.

"Good to see you, Josie," she said.

She reached into her purse, pulled out some coins and distributed them between the children like carefully calculated peace offerings.

"Go find some sweets. Stay together, and Todd..." she fixed her eldest with a meaningful look, "keep an eye on Benji, will you?"

Todd rolled his eyes but nodded.

"Come on, squirt," he said to his little brother.

"How's Todd doing these days?" I asked.

Sally adjusted her ponytail, waiting until the children were safely out of earshot.

"Some days are better than others," she admitted. "He doesn't talk much, but he misses his dad, you know? And I know he still has nightmares about the murder and the kidnap." She paused. "I'm so grateful that you rescued him."

I gave her hand a gentle squeeze.

That event weighed heavily on me as well. You don't forget stopping a bullet with magic.

Sally exhaled, her face brightening.

"But spending time with Jamie seems to help," she said.

"Jamie?" I raised an eyebrow.

"PC Waverley," she clarified, blushing. "One of the officers from the kidnap."

"Oh, Jamie," I teased, drawing out the name with exaggerated delight. "Didn't I see him arrive not five minutes ago? I didn't realise you and Officer Waverley were on a first-name basis."

Sally blushed so furiously I half expected smoke to rise from her ears.

"It's not like that," she protested, maybe a little too much. "He's just been... really great with Todd."

I nodded solemnly.

"And it's good Todd has someone to talk to," Sally went on. "A male role model."

I paused, then grinned. "Especially one with a uniform and handcuffs?"

"Josie!" Sally gasped, her cheeks blazing red.

I laughed.

"I'm sorry. I couldn't resist. But seriously, I'm thrilled for you. You deserve some happiness after..." My voice softened. "After losing Martin in the accident."

Sally swallowed, nodding.

"Me and Jamie are friends," she insisted again. "And you've some nerve. You're always with Tom."

Now it was my turn to blush.

"Tom's been a rock while I've been getting Briarwood Gables ready for guests," I blustered. "And it's not like *that* with us, either. We're just friends too."

It wasn't untrue.

We were friends. Good friends.

But truthfully, I wasn't sure what Tom and I were.

During the renovations, we'd worked side-by-side. We'd shared laughter and frustrations, and he'd taught me to cook Spiced Vegetable Chowder: my grandmother's recipe passed down through him like some culinary inheritance.

And okay, yes, he had the kindest brown eyes and a chest I couldn't forget after that incident on my first day, when he'd emerged from my bathroom wearing nothing but a towel and a slightly startled expression.

He'd spoken about his late wife, lost to cancer years ago. He knew how Gary had gone bankrupt and fled the country without so much as a goodbye, leaving me with an endless supply of headaches in the form of solicitor's letters.

Of course, he also knew that, technically, I was still married.

But now I had Gary's divorce papers...

Well, that was a thought I wasn't quite ready to unpack.

And certainly not while standing with Sally in the middle of the village green.

Luckily, Sally had other gossip on her mind. She lowered her voice. "Anyway, I spoke to Jamie and guess what? He says they're treating Ron Burrows's death as suspicious."

"Told you," purred Einstein, his tail waving from side to side triumphantly.

"You mean, like murder?" I leaned closer. "What did he say?"

Chapter 7

"WELL, JAMIE WASN'T ABLE to tell me the exact details, obviously," Sally confided. "But he did mention that things weren't as straightforward as they looked. Apparently, they suspect Ronald Burrows didn't die of a heart attack, and there's talk it might have 'something' to do with Eva!"

"Eva!" I gasped.

Sally grabbed my arm like a woman stopping a runaway horse. "Keep your voice down," she hissed.

I exhaled sharply. "There's no way Eva would kill Ronald," I muttered.

Sally tilted her head to one side. "Well, people are bringing up the 'Floral Disaster' from last year."

"The what?"

"Oh, it was before you arrived in Briarvale," Sally explained. "Ron knocked over Eva's floral display right before the judging at the flower show and had the nerve to claim it looked better that way. Eva was livid. Worse still, Ron kept making jokes about it for months. Called her 'Petal' once in a Parish Council meeting."

I shrugged. "That's... unfortunate, and not very tactful of him," I said. "But it hardly seems a motive to kill the man."

"No," Sally agreed. "But it's the sort of thing that builds up over time, isn't it? You know, death by a thousand paper cuts. And Eva has always been... intense about village traditions."

"I'd want to kill him if he called me Petal," put in Einstein, his tail flicking irritably.

I tried to keep my face straight.

"Well, I saw Eva and Ronald arguing earlier," I said. "And Sylvia told me that Eva was upset last year when her hanging basket only placed second in the annual flower show which Ronald judged, too."

Sally nodded wisely. "See. It all adds up."

"I suppose," I agreed, stepping forward as the queue shuffled along.

I was next in line for the lemonade van, the scent of freshly squeezed citrus drifting towards me temptingly.

Sally glanced round. "I should go and find where my lot have got to," she said, searching the crowd for a tell-tale trail of mischief.

"Let me know if you hear anything else," I urged her. "Especially from Jamie."

Sally nodded. "Of course. Though I think even he's in the dark about most of it."

She gave me a quick smile, then disappeared into the sea of festival-goers.

I bent down next to Einstein, so people in the line wouldn't guess I was talking to my cat.

"Do you think Eva killed Ronald?" I asked.

"Appearances can be deceiving," Einstein remarked cryptically, his tail twitching with interest. "Though, in this case, I rather doubt our esteemed Eva is capable of murder. Especially not this murder. Too messy. Too unplanned. She'd have a colour-coded spreadsheet and three committee meetings first to decide how to dispose of the body."

I bit back a smile. The situation was serious, but Einstein's assessment of Eva's character wasn't far off the mark.

I bought my lemonade and walked over to where I'd left Tom, who was now rolling a ball for Murphy along the grass. Murphy was chasing it like his life depended on it, pouncing with laser focus, tail wagging furiously as though it were the most critical mission in the world.

Einstein eyed him with disdain.

"Ah, retrieving objects that do absolutely nothing. The pinnacle of canine intelligence," he drawled. "If only he was able to apply that focus to something worthwhile... like not drooling everywhere."

I tried not to grin as I sat down beside Tom.

"Feel better?" he asked, taking the ball from Murphy's slobbery grip.

"Yes, thanks."

I took a slow sip of lemonade, letting the coolness clear my thoughts before turning to Tom.

"Sally told me something interesting."

"Oh?"

Tom tossed the ball again, and Murphy shot after it with unwavering enthusiasm.

"Apparently, they've ruled out anything to do with Ronald's heart, and..." I hesitated, lowering my voice, "and there's a rumour it might have something to do with Eva."

Tom turned to look at me. Finally, giving me his full attention.

"No!"

I nodded, watching as Murphy snatched up the ball and paraded his soggy prize back to us proudly.

"Sally said Eva and Ronald have a long-running feud. Some incident that happened at last year's flower show. And, well..." I gestured towards the HoneyPot, "we both saw them arguing earlier."

Tom exhaled slowly, as Murphy dropped the ball at his feet again. "Yes, but Eva? No way."

There didn't seem anything else to add.

I turned my attention back to the stage where the paramedics and the police were still working on the scene, their movements determined.

DI Holloway looked particularly frazzled, jaw tight, shoulders stiff. He had the expression of a man who already knew the investigation was going to be an uphill battle.

The village green hummed with movement: dancers lingering, spectators milling, and the afternoon stallholders hurriedly packing up their things, eager to slip away before they got entangled in police procedure. As if the murder of Ronald Burrows was a minor inconvenience.

By now, more officers had arrived. Working with methodical efficiency, they photographed the scene and bagged evidence. However, their attempts to corral the witnesses and take statements were much less successful.

I stood back, sipping my lemonade, noting DI Holloway's growing frustration as he attempted to restore control to a situation that refused to be contained.

Next thing, the microphone crackled to life.

"Ahem."

DI Holloway winced as his voice rang out, oddly thin through the speaker system.

"Ladies and gentlemen."

He cleared his throat again, the mic distorting the sound into the over-loud grumble of a disgruntled walrus.

"This is... Detective Inspector Holloway."

Another pause.

The pause of a man who would rather be interrogating suspects than addressing an entire, uncooperative village.

"I need everyone to remain on the green until further notice."

A murmur of unease rippled through the crowd.

Holloway shifted on his feet, muttered something near the mic that was too low to catch, then exhaled sharply.

"If you witnessed anything suspicious regarding Ronald Burrows before his collapse, please report to my officers immediately."

Another pause.

Someone coughed.

Holloway looked as though he wanted to throw the microphone into the nearest hedge. He was clearly wondering if glaring at the crowd would be more effective.

He turned to one of his officers with renewed focus. "Start identifying key witnesses. Lock down movement near the crime scene."

His orders were relayed to the entire village before he remembered to switch off the microphone.

I took another sip of my drink, as the police struggled against pure logistics.

Too many people. Too many shifting accounts. Too much ground to cover before crucial details got trampled under festival chaos.

But DI Holloway had left the stage. Now he was heading straight toward us.

Murphy noticed him too. The ball dropped from his mouth, all games forgotten, as he positioned himself between Tom and the detective, a low growl rumbling in his throat.

Tom laid a firm hand on Murphy's collar, sending me a knowing glance.

"Seems Murphy hasn't forgiven Holloway for arresting me last time there was a murder," he said.

"For once, the dog is displaying sound judgment," said Einstein, his tail swishing back and forth. "Shame he has to spoil it by chewing shoes."

DI Holloway reached us, his gaze flicking from Tom to me.

"Ms Appleton. Mr Carver," said the DI, with a look that felt like it should come with a warning label.

I straightened.

"Detective," I replied, unsure if I was being accused of something already.

"You were present for the whole competition?" he asked.

"Yes."

"Did you notice anything unusual about Ronald Burrows?"

I shook my head. "I'm afraid I didn't know him," I said truthfully. "This was the first time I'd met the man."

"But you witnessed his disagreement with Eva Henshaw earlier?"

The question caught me off guard.

I *was* there. And I couldn't lie, even if it implicated Eva.

"Yes."

DI Holloway's eyes narrowed.

"So, you can confirm they had a *heated* argument?"

I hesitated. "Umm... they argued," I said carefully. "But I'm sure Eva had no part in the death of poor Ronald Burrows."

"You seem very certain of that," he observed sceptically.

"Well, Eva can be prickly, but I can't imagine her hurting anyone."

And I meant it.

"Few people can imagine their neighbours are murderers," DI Holloway replied, his tone professionally detached. "Yet somebody is."

He turned to Tom. Their conversation, held over the top of Murphy's head, was brief and similarly professional.

However, before DI Holloway strode away, he fixed me with a hard stare. "One more thing, Ms Appleton," he said, voice like the snap of a closing case file. "I trust you will leave the investigation to the trained professionals this time."

I gave him my best sweet-but-suspiciously-innocent smile.

"Why, of course. This has nothing to do with me."

The DI studied me a moment longer, as if trying to decide whether to believe me. Then, with a curt nod, he strode away.

"Looks like he's got his sights set on Eva," Tom groaned. "Poor woman."

"He can't seriously believe she'd murder anyone," I said.

And just like that, the case of the poisoned judge had truly begun.

Chapter 8

AFTER LEAVING US, DI Holloway wove his way through the crowd, then up the steps onto the stage. Immediately, an officer scurried over, carrying the box that had held the judges' results.

Einstein must be right about the poison.

Holloway and the officer spoke in hushed voices, clipped and efficient.

A ripple of tension.

Murmurs.

Bracing silence.

DI Holloway approached Eva, who still stood rigidly near the stage. Florence, as always, hovered anxiously at her side.

Even from a distance, I could see the detective's expression harden as Eva spoke, her hands moving in sharp, defensive gestures.

"That doesn't look good," Tom muttered.

He was right. The conversation between Eva and DI Holloway had turned decidedly confrontational. Eva's voice rose louder so that fragments carried across the green.

"Ridiculous assumption... I've known Ronald for years... the very idea... complete overreaction."

The detective's response was too quiet to hear, but whatever he said stopped Eva cold. Her already pale features blanched to the colour of paper, and for the first time since I'd met her, she seemed lost for words. Florence clutched at her arm. Her perpetually worried expression was now genuinely distressed.

Holloway gave a curt nod to his officers, but Eva flinched as though he'd slapped her across the face.

"Mrs Henshaw," Holloway said, his voice firm and loud enough for those nearest to hear. "I need you to come with us for questioning."

There it was. Not handcuffs, not a dramatic announcement, but everyone on the village green knew what it meant.

The police suspected Eva of the murder of Ronald Burrows.

Another murmur rippled through the crowd.

Two officers led Eva toward a waiting squad car. Suddenly she looked smaller, older, her usual rigid posture giving way to a slight stoop. Florence made to follow her, but Jamie Waverley gently turned her away.

I watched as the car containing Eva pulled off the green, its exit observed by clusters of villagers with expressions ranging from shock to barely concealed fascination.

The afternoon sun was still bright, but the festive atmosphere of the competition had been thoroughly extinguished, replaced by a buzz of speculation and unease.

As the car disappeared down the lane, a sharp tut came from behind me.

Percy Henshaw stood ramrod straight, his Whirligig Wobblers costume, for once, not quite perfect. His sash sat twisted, his hat tilted a fraction off-centre, and one bell on his leg hung lower than the others.

At his feet, Charlie had spotted Murphy. His little ears twitched, and, his whole body quivering with wild delight, he trotted over with the confidence of an animal who assumed everyone would love him... and usually did. Murphy gave him a polite tail wag in return, entirely indifferent to Charlie's enthusiasm but far too polite to show it.

For a blissful moment, all seemed well.

Until Charlie turned his head and spotted Einstein.

Einstein, who had been sitting observing the officers at the judges' table with dignified composure, barely had time to react before Charlie lunged forward in a flurry of barking and scrabbling paws.

Murphy, recognising the imminent disaster, wisely removed himself from the situation by retiring behind Tom, while Einstein vaulted onto a nearby chair, tail puffed up, eyes blazing.

Fuelled by the kind of excitement that defied all reason, Charlie bounced after him, tangling the lead round Percy's legs in the process.

Percy let out an exasperated sigh, unwinding Charlie's lead with practised efficiency and guiding the tiny whirlwind back to order.

Charlie squirmed in protest, but Percy held firm, adjusting his already-askew waistcoat as though this disruption was merely another test of his patience.

Then, without looking at the wriggling Shorkie, he murmured, "I know, Charliekins. We're all upset about Mummy going off in that nasty old police car. But she won't be gone for long, I'm sure of it."

Charlie whined at the mention of 'Mummy', his ears drooping.

Percy sighed again, glancing at the dog properly this time. "You'll have to behave, you know. Causing a kerfuffle in front of these police officers isn't going to help Mummy, is it?"

Einstein, still perched on the chair, flicked his tail in silent fury.

Percy straightened, casting a critical glance across the village green as though the sheer disorder pained him. "This is simply unacceptable," he announced to no-one in particular. "My wife has run this contest with the precision of a well-oiled machine for thirty years, and the authorities carry her off like some common hooligan? There'll be consequences for this, I'm sure."

I exchanged a glance with Tom.

Percy's outrage wasn't theatrical, it was practical. He had never met a problem that couldn't be resolved with efficiency, timing, and an adherence to rules. And yet, here he was, faced with the complete breakdown of order, and his outfit looked as rattled as he was.

I turned to face him. "I'm certain it's all a misunderstanding," I said carefully, while Charlie twisted himself in knots around Percy's ankles.

Percy sniffed. "Well, someone had better sort it out promptly. As if my wife would ever be part of such a thing..." He shook his head. "Utterly preposterous. My wife of all people! And what would be her reason?" he continued. "She was in the middle of getting Ronald replaced. She'd been collecting complaints about him for months. Documenting every harsh comment, every questionable scoring decision."

That got my attention.

"She was building a case?" I gasped.

"She had a folder." Percy lowered his voice and leaned closer. "'Burrows's Transgressions'. Cross-referenced quotes. You know the sort."

It sounded very like Eva.

"She was planning to present it at the next Morris Dancing Association meeting," Percy told me.

"So she didn't need to kill him if she was about to win anyway," I reasoned.

"Exactly," said Percy. "She was days away from victory. She wouldn't have killed him before that. She would have liked to see him squirm."

And that, more than anything, confirmed my suspicions: Eva Henshaw was many things. But a murderer? Not a chance.

Percy spotted Florence and headed off in her direction with Charlie in tow without so much as a goodbye.

Tom turned to me. "Do you believe Eva did it?"

"No," I blurted. "Do you?"

"Nah. Eva's formidable, no question. But a murderer? That's a stretch."

"Exactly," I agreed, relieved he shared my view.

"Though if anyone in the village would get away with it, it's Eva," Tom added with a wry smile.

I shook my head. "Even Eva wouldn't think she could murder a judge during a Morris dancing competition with dozens of witnesses present and not get caught. She's bossy and opinionated, and occasionally tyrannical in her approach to village life, but she's not stupid."

In the distance, the church bells chimed the half-hour, the familiar sound somehow ominous in the tense atmosphere that had settled on the scene.

"The question is, if it wasn't Eva," I said slowly, "then who was it?"

And how was I going to prove it, before Briarvale's self-appointed queen found herself permanently dethroned?

I tightened my grip on my lemonade.

Because I knew Eva.

And I knew Holloway was making a mistake.

"I have to help her," I said. Ignoring DI Holloway's advice to not get involved.

The trouble was, I had no idea how.

"You solved the case last time," said Tom encouragingly.

Einstein pressed close to my leg. "You'll figure it out," he mewed.

Chapter 9

W HILE WE WAITED FOR the police to get round to
taking our statements, Tom and I sat on the grass
mulling over what we knew.

"If there was poison on the envelope that Ronald Burrows
sealed his voting into..." I started.

"Why do you think he was poisoned?" Tom interrupted.

I froze, a hot flush creeping up my neck.

"Oops," said Einstein, flicking his ears. "Busted."

"Umm... Sally said Jamie Waverley told her it was a suspicious death," I answered, which was true. Tom wasn't to
know she hadn't been specific about exactly how suspicious.

I had to be more careful.

"Oh, tell Tom your cat told you," chortled Einstein. "I'd
love to see his face."

I glowered at him.

Tom looked mildly confused. "O...K..." he said slowly. "Sorry I interrupted. Carry on."

I took a breath, grateful Tom wasn't pushing the issue.

"So," I continued, "if someone poisoned the envelope, we need to know who put all the envelopes on the table."

"I guess that would be Eva," said Tom thoughtfully.

We both looked at each other.

That didn't help Eva's case.

"Florence would be able to tell us for certain," I said.

We searched through the swirl of villagers and dancers until Tom spotted her talking animatedly to a police officer, her arms waving, the ribbons on her Whirligig Wobblers costume fluttering with each movement.

"Seems I wasn't the only one who thought Florence might know something," I said. "But DI Holloway's beaten me to it. I'll have to catch her later. But if we're assuming Eva didn't kill him, who else might have wanted to?"

Tom gestured at the assembled crowd of dancers and villagers. "Take your pick," he said.

"Well, yes. Ronald Burrows was universally disliked, had a tongue sharper than my grandmother's carving knife, and it appeared he managed to insult practically every Morris dancer within a fifty-mile radius. But wanting to kill him is a whole other level." I stifled a sigh. "Do you know anything else about him?"

Tom thought for a moment. "He came from up north, Manchester or somewhere. He moved here with his wife when he retired. I think he was an accountant."

"Maybe he was a dodgy accountant and someone he embezzled got their revenge?" I suggested.

"Maybe," said Tom. "Although he's been retired for years. Seems a long time to hold a grudge."

"Maybe they only just found him," I said. "You know, he might have been in witness protection, or something."

Tom laughed. "You should be *writing* murder mysteries, not trying to solve them." He shook his head. "And honestly, they didn't seem to be in hiding. Margaret, his wife, really got involved in village life. She danced with the Wobblers. Lovely woman. And she dragged Ronald along with her. He wasn't much of a dancer, mind, so that didn't last long. But he learned everything about the tradition to help her. After she passed, he carried on with the judging."

I tried to imagine how bad at dancing Ronald had to have been to get himself thrown out of the Whirligig Wobblers.

"The point is," I sighed, "everyone appears to have a motive to want him gone. The real question is, who had the opportunity to make that happen?"

My thoughts were interrupted by the arrival of PC Jamie Waverley, clipboard in hand.

"Hi Tom. Josie," he said, wiping a bead of sweat running from under his police hat. "I only need to jot down your names and addresses, and what you witnessed, and then you're free to go."

Jamie always had an easy-going manner, despite the uniform. He was exactly the kind of man that matched Sally. Decent. Cheerful. Solid.

I almost said something about it, but Jamie looked hot and bothered enough already, and I had the feeling that the last thing he needed was me bringing up his dating life while he was half-melting.

Jamie wrote down our details, then he got up to leave.

"Nice seeing you again," he said. "Shame it's not under better circumstances." He shifted the clipboard under his arm and added, "I still remember that cake you gave me when they had me guarding the crime scene at your house." His grin turned a little hopeful. "Really good."

And suddenly, I knew exactly how to move forward with my investigation.

Cookies.

I needed to bake cookies.

Not any old cookies mind. The special kind my grandmother had made: the kind that loosened tongues and refreshed memories and encouraged truths. If ever there was a time for a bit of magical baking, surely a village murder called for it.

"We should head back to Briarwood," Tom said, pulling me from my thoughts. " I need to sort the animals out, and some of your guests will be returning to change for the evening's entertainment."

"You're right," I said to Tom, jumping to my feet purposefully. "And I need to do some baking."

"Now you're talking," said Einstein. He'd been sitting innocently by my feet licking one paw, now he stood up and stretched.

"Baking?" Tom repeated, surprised. "There'll be plenty of food at the post-competition party."

"I know, but..." I hesitated, searching for an explanation that wouldn't sound completely mad. "It helps me think. And I'd like to bring a homemade dish to the festival supper. A contribution."

Tom's expression softened, the lines around his eyes crinkling with understanding. "You're so like your grandmother," he said quietly. "Always baking when she had something on her mind. Used to say she'd solve all the world's problems with the right combination of flour and butter."

"Did she?"

A lump formed unexpectedly in my throat. I'd never known my grandmother, so each new revelation about her was a gift; a thread connecting me to her across the years.

"Oh yes," Tom confirmed. "Beatrix was a firm believer in the therapeutic qualities of baking. And eating," he added with a pat to his stomach. "I can attest to that second part personally."

"I guess it was the magical element that really helped," Einstein added.

I laughed.

Tom smiled ruefully. "Course, since I've been on this healthy eating thing with Dr Hale, I've been keeping off the sweet stuff."

Tom had said this before, and I was glad, otherwise, how would I stop him from sampling all my magical baking?

"Right, come on, Murphy," said Tom, giving the dog's fur an affectionate ruffle. "Let's go home, shall we?"

We piled into Tom's pickup. The seats had seen better days, the leather cracked in places, but the engine hummed into life with the reassuring rumble of machinery that had been well-maintained despite its years. Einstein settled onto my lap, his body unusually tense as he stared out the window at the receding scene of the crime.

"Do you think they'll cancel the evening's events?" I asked as we bumped along the lane toward Briarwood Gables. "Now that they have a murder case?"

"Cancel the band?" Tom's hands were steady on the wheel, his profile thoughtful in the slanting afternoon light. "Not likely. I saw them setting up at the pub earlier, and then there are all the food vans turning up. There'd be a riot if the hog roast didn't show. Besides," he shot me a sideways glance, "nothing, not even a murder, can stop the dancers from drinking and celebrating. Especially the winning team."

"It seems... disrespectful," I said, thinking of Ronald Burrows lying forgotten while celebrations continued.

"I suppose," Tom conceded. "But life goes on, doesn't it? Been going on in this village for hundreds of years, through wars and plagues and all sorts of calamities. Morris dancers have probably been drinking to their victories since before the Normans arrived."

I smiled despite myself. Tom had a way of putting things in perspective, of making even a murder seem like simply another bend in the long road of village history.

I never got tired of seeing Briarwood Gables, and tonight the honey stone walls were glowing in the warm light of early evening.

"How long are you going to be?" Tom asked, parking the truck by the garden wall.

"A couple of hours," I told him. "I've been brushing up my baking skills."

Tom smiled. "Don't rush," he said. "Some problems need more flour than others, I expect."

"He's almost right about that," put in Einstein, leaping gracefully off the dashboard onto the wall. "But flour isn't the active ingredient in your pastries," he chuckled.

"I'm planning on returning to the village about eight," Tom was saying.

"I'll be ready for then," I promised.

Tom headed off with Murphy to feed Hetty and Betty, the chickens, and try to tempt the sheep, goat and ducks back inside for the night. Meanwhile, Einstein and I made our way inside the house.

The hallway of Briarwood Gables welcomed me with familiar creaks and cool shadows, the ancient wooden floorboards groaning gently under my feet as if greeting an old friend.

Pointedly ignoring the envelope on the hall table containing Gary's divorce papers, I checked out the grandfather clock.

The hands still pointed at 4.20.

Good. Hopefully, that meant no more disasters were going to happen today.

Some of the guests had also returned, and it felt odd hearing the sound of voices drifting from upstairs. The Morris dancing competition had given them more to think about than anyone had bargained for, and they were discussing the day's dramatic events in hushed, excited tones.

I guess I had to get used to not being alone, now the house was a B&B.

"Right," said Einstein, padding down the hallway, a cat on a mission. "Which magical delicacies are going to be needed to solve this case?"

Chapter 10

THE KITCHEN WAITED AT the end of the corridor, cool and quiet. Its stone floor and exposed beams were unchanged since my ancestors, the three original Stanton sisters, had built it over a hundred years before, presumably between bouts of spell-casting and scone-baking.

"Let's get to work," I said, closing the door behind us and turning to Einstein.

"What's the plan?" he asked, jumping onto the central island with the grace of an Olympic gymnast.

"Truth-Whispering Muffins? Memory-Sparking Shortbread? And Loose-Tongue Toffee?" I announced. "The full magical menu."

"What? All three?" he mewed, half-alarmed, half intrigued.

"Well, we don't know exactly what we need for the investigation yet," I reasoned, reaching for the flour canister. "So it's best to be prepared."

Einstein considered this. "Practical," he approved. "Your grandmother would be impressed. Possibly concerned, but impressed."

I smiled as I reached for my grandmother's recipe book from its place on the top shelf. I flipped straight to the page for Truth-Whispering Muffins. Since arriving at Briarwood Gables, I'd done a lot of magical baking, and I was fairly confident today's batches would turn out correctly, even under the pressure of the murder investigation.

Through the window, I saw Geoff and June wandering along the path towards the river, together with some of the other Green Stags and a couple of the Crimson Bells. I was quietly relieved to know Tom was over that way seeing to the animals. I wouldn't like one of my guests to run into Mr Tuppyhead, Tom's goat, without backup.

I turned my attention to the recipe, running my finger down the list of magical ingredients.

"Gossamer Sugar," I read aloud. "Encourages truthfulness... gently."

I looked at Einstein expectantly.

"Storeroom," he supplied, flicking his tail. "Middle shelf, behind the door, and don't mistake it for Stardust Sweetener, unless you want people sobbing about their childhood traumas."

Sure enough, a pale blue jar sat on the shelf, the sugar inside scattering the light in a soft, silvery glint.

"How much do I use?" I asked, unscrewing the lid.

Einstein hopped onto the table and peered at the recipe. "Enough to coax out the truth, but not so much they confess to stealing a library book in 1987."

"Not super specific," I muttered.

"Use a teaspoon full."

"Got it."

I grinned and measured it in, then turned to stir the batter.

"Thirty-three times. Exactly," said Einstein.

"Does it really have to be exact?"

He fixed me with the kind of look cats reserve for humans who have disappointed them deeply.

"Yes. Of course it does," I said, and I started counting under my breath as I wove the enchantment into the simple ingredients in my bowl.

My magic is not the flashy, fireworks-in-the-sky kind. It's quiet. Subtle. The sort that hums beneath the surface. A gift passed down through generations of Stanton women. It doesn't demand: it nudges. A whisper of the ancient Stanton gift folded into flour and sugar.

Fifteen.

Sixteen.

At seventeen, Einstein yowled, "The oven! It's getting too hot!"

I yelped, the spoon slipped, and a puff of flour exploded into the air. The bowl jerked violently, turning my careful spell into a swirly disaster.

"Brilliant." He groaned. "Now instead of quiet confessions, people might start declaring their undying love to their postman. Or confessing to taking extra biscuits at church garden parties."

I turned down the dial on the oven with a scowl. "Hey, don't blame me," I huffed. "You're the one who was wailing like a banshee. You scared me half to death."

To be fair, Einstein did look vaguely apologetic. He retreated to the chair and curled his tail round himself.

I finished stirring the muffins with as much care as I could manage, spooned the batter into muffin tins, and slid them into the oven, muttering a silent prayer to the god of baking.

"You know," Einstein said, "this is quite the baptism by fire for your first summer in Briarvale. Most new witches get a year or two to practise spells and ease into village politics. You? Two murders in three months. Has to be a record."

"Lucky me," I murmured, turning to the recipe for Memory-Sparking Shortbread.

I scanned the instructions until I landed on the magical ingredient.

"Echoing Vanilla," I murmured.

Einstein nodded. "Retrieves memories, but only if the subject actually wants to remember. It's behind the bottles of cobwebs on the right hand wall. Don't knock over the Pickled Moonbeams on the way. They're temperamental."

The vial of vanilla was small and delicate, the liquid inside shimmering like moonlight trapped in glass.

Carefully, I pulled out the stopper.

"One drop," Einstein warned. "Exactly one. And you need to speak a memory aloud as you fold it into the dough."

"Like... any memory?" I asked warily.

Einstein gave me a look like I'd served him curdled cream. "Well, not yesterday's weather, Josie. Something personal. Something with a heartbeat."

I took a slow breath, the vial poised over the mixing bowl.

A house. One of many. A place that never quite became a home. As the child of an army contractor, I'd collected new postcodes the way other kids collected football stickers. We'd been there an hour, but I already knew the pattern: boxes unpacked halfway, furniture positioned but never settled, blank walls waiting for art that never came.

I remembered sitting on the edge of my bed, placing my worn, stuffed cat on the pillow. His name was Whiskers, though his actual whiskers had vanished when my father decided he needed a spin in the washing machine. He was threadbare, lopsided, and loyal. The closest thing to a pet my father ever allowed.

Now, of course, I had a real cat. One with opinions and sass.

"You look nothing like Whiskers," I said to Einstein.

The vanilla glowed briefly as I folded it into the mixture, the magic catching the weight of the memory and tucking it neatly into the ingredients.

Einstein gave an approving nod. "That'll do," he said.

Feeling oddly sentimental, I shaped the soft dough and placed the shortbread into the oven, the scent of warm spice already curling into the warm kitchen air like a spell of its own.

Finally, I turned my attention to the Loose-Tongue Toffee, which required a pinch of crushed Silverleaf to be stirred into the sugar mixture whilst chanting "Tell ten tiny truthful tales".

That sounded easy enough.

Einstein patted the drawer where my grandmother's cooking thermometer lived, then he settled on the windowsill to resume his role as fluffy grey supervisor.

"The secret," he instructed, "is to cool the toffee gradually. If you rush it, people won't be able to stop talking."

"That's kind of the point," I said, pouring in the sugar.

Einstein gave me a look. "No, Josie. I mean, they won't. Stop. Talking. Ever."

I swallowed. "Okay. Cool slowly. Got it."

Repeating "Tell ten tiny truthful tales" over and over as I stirred was a tongue-twister that required careful concentration, and I was glad when it was time to finally take the pan from the heat.

I was about to pour the toffee into a tray, when a commotion erupted outside the window.

Loud shouting. Frantic footsteps. And the unmistakable honk of a triumphant goose.

I turned round in time to see Agatha, the goose, tearing down the garden path, wings flapping, a silver pocket watch dangling from her beak.

Hot on her tail came Tom, three Green Stags, and two Crimson Bells, all sprinting faster than Olympic hopefuls, arms flailing, voices bellowing accusations about "theft" and "that blasted bird".

Agatha, however, looked delighted. The feathered thief honked in triumph and flashed the pocket watch in the sunlight, flaunting her latest haul.

Startled by the unexpected mayhem, Einstein sat up too fast, misjudged his footing, and toppled off the windowsill. In a flailing attempt to recover, he bashed into my elbow, bounced off the table, and collided with the bag of flour, which exploded into a billowing haze of white powder.

There was a long, shocked pause as the cloud settled, coating every surface in fine dust.

Two amber eyes blinked at me from a flour-coated fuzzball. Another pause.

"We will never speak of this," said Einstein flatly.

Outside, Agatha gave one last victorious honk, pocket watch still clutched in her beak, and the chase continued past the garden gate.

That did it.

I collapsed against the counter, laughing until my sides ached, barely managing to pour the toffee onto the cooling tray without incident.

The muffins and shortbread were ready, and their delicious scents filled the air like an enchantment. Vanilla and sugar, and a tiny whiff of magic.

Einstein, still ghost white, licked the flour from his paws. "Well, at least something went right today," he said.

I surveyed the results of our magical bake-athon; everything lined up and ready for the post-festival celebrations.

Would they work? Would my enchanted treats help uncover who had decided Ronald Burrows had judged his final Morris dancing competition?

Or would I accidentally cause an epidemic of confession and chaos?

There was only one way to find out.

Chapter 11

ONCE THE TOFFEE HAD cooled, I snapped it into pieces and began packing all the freshly baked goodies into a black tin decorated with faded gold flowers and stars. It was the one which, according to Einstein, my grandmother had used for exactly this purpose: carrying her magical baking into the world.

I was finishing up, when the kitchen door creaked open, and Liam Cardew bobbed his head round.

The scowl I'd seen earlier, back when the Green Stags had been announced as winners rather than the Crimson Bells, had vanished. Now he was all easy smiles and summer confidence, dressed in skinny jeans and a white t-shirt that showed off a golden tan. The bold war paint from the afternoon's performance had mostly been scrubbed away, leaving only a faint crimson smudge along his hairline, as if the battle had been washed off but the defeat was not entirely forgotten.

"Ah, I've found the source of that delicious smell," he teased, his voice lilting like a man with a rehearsed pick-up line which he had no shame in using. "I can never resist the smell of fresh baking."

"Guilty as charged," I replied.

Liam struck me as the kind of guy who'd flirt with the postwoman, sweet-talk the vicar, and charm the pants off a parking warden.

He'd also been incredibly angry when his team lost.

Angry enough to kill the judge?

Possibly.

Either way, he was a perfect test subject for my magical bakes.

"Care for a taste?" I offered, gesturing to the open tin of toffees.

Liam grinned like a toddler with an all-access pass to the sweet shop. "Don't mind if I do," he replied, selecting a piece and popping it into his mouth.

His eyes fluttered shut as though he was having a religious experience in caramel form.

"Wow! These are dangerously good," he enthused. "What do you put in them?"

I tapped my finger on the side of my nose. "Sorry. Trade secret."

Einstein paused mid-leg-lick. "Smooth answer," he purred.

"Terrible thing about the judge," I said, casually leaning on the table as if we were gossiping about the weather.

"Yeah..." Liam's tone grew quieter. "Bit of a shock, alright."

Einstein shook the last of the flour from his paw, his eyes narrowing. "Don't push him too fast," he warned me. "Give the spell time to work."

Liam was still licking the toffee from his teeth. "Still... can't say I'm heartbroken," he added. "It's a relief, in a way. No debts. No more arguing."

I frowned. "Debts?"

He only paused for a heartbeat, but it was there, the flicker in his eyes, the tension settling in his jaw.

"Oh... you know," he said, his voice lighter now. "Old grudges. Nothing serious."

"Old grudges?" I echoed, sweet and innocent as the toffee itself. "Now you've got me curious."

But I'd blown it. I'd been too eager to dig for clues.

Liam's smile was back, polished and guarded. "Let's say Ronald Burrows wasn't known for letting things go. Ever." He straightened up. "But the guy's dead now, so 'let bygones' and all that."

I looked at him, annoyed with myself that my impatience had spoiled the magic.

Debts and grudges were interesting, but were they relevant to the murder?

Before I could say more, the door swung open, and Tom walked in, followed by Murphy. He'd changed into the black jeans he wore when he was going out and a blue shirt, and my mind flipped back to Sally's earlier comment about how much time I spent with him. He wasn't flashy, but he was good-looking in a rugged sort of way and there was something reassuringly solid about him. He wasn't the sort to desert his wife and leave her to sort out the mess.

That thought slipped out before I could stop it.

But hey, I never imagined Gary was that sort either. I guess you can never tell.

Tom stopped short when he saw Liam. "The Crimson Bells are invading the kitchen now, are they?" He was out of breath, likely from chasing Agatha, but there was a subtle edge to his tone.

"Can you blame me?" Liam said with a cheeky wink at me. "The smell of home-baking called to me." And he confidently helped himself to another piece of toffee.

Tom took a step towards him, and Einstein sat bolt upright.

"Hey! You shouldn't have let him take two!" Einstein yowled. "You'll have him talking in rhyme if he keeps eating it."

I looked at him, horrified.

Was that a thing?

Einstein nodded sagely in answer to my unspoken question. "I once saw a village councillor recite her grocery list in limerick form after only three toffees."

I slammed the lid onto the tin and stuffed it into my bag before Liam came back for more.

"The Crimson Bells did an impressive performance this afternoon," Tom was saying to Liam. The words were polite, but somehow they lacked his usual warmth.

What was going on?

"Thanks." Liam sighed through a mouthful of toffee. "Not good enough to win though. But speaking of performances, I saw you lot chasing that goose earlier. Best dance I've seen all day."

Tom turned to the sink and started scrubbing his hands vigorously. "Don't remind me," he groaned.

"Did you get the watch back off Agatha?" I asked.

"Eventually," he said. "Murphy cornered her in the orchard and barked until she dropped it."

Murphy's tail thumped against the floor with the joyful excitement of a folk dancer's boots at the mention of his victory over Agatha's thieving.

Liam swallowed the last of the toffee and stretched his arms lazily. "Well, The Briar and Thorn is calling," he said. "Time for a well-earned pint... or three." He winked at me again. "Thanks for the toffee, Josie."

And with that, he sauntered out.

I waited until the door swung shut before I turned to Tom, noticing his shoulders relax again.

"Liam talked about debts and grudges with Ronald Burrows," I said excitedly. "Any idea what he meant?"

Tom shook his head. "Not a clue. Sorry."

"It sounds like a motive for murder though, don't you think?"

Tom dried his hands thoughtfully. "Could be, I suppose." He looked at the container of goodies packed into my bag. "You made enough goodies to feed half of the village, Sherlock Appleton," he teased. "Did the baking help clear your head?"

"Perfectly," I said.

"That's good," he said. "I imagine people will be grateful for these later, especially after a few pints at The Briar and Thorn. Let's go back and see if you can sniff out any more clues." He grinned. "Or you could simply relax and enjoy listening to the band?"

"Not a chance," I objected.

Already I was planning how to distribute my enchanted treats strategically at the evening's celebrations. I needed to watch reactions carefully, and piece together the puzzle of who had decided a Morris dance judge deserved to die. But I wasn't going to explain that to Tom.

"Thought not," he grinned.

I hoisted my bag onto my shoulder.

"I'll grab a jacket for later," I told Tom. "And meet you at the truck."

As I walked through the hallway, I checked the time on the grandfather clock.

The hands still showed 4.20.

I let out a sigh of relief.

Satisfied there was no fresh doom on the horizon, I took that as a good omen and hurried outside.

We piled into Tom's pickup. Me riding shotgun with my tin of magical baking clutched on my knee, Murphy in the back and Einstein perched in his usual place on the dashboard.

The sun was disappearing over the hills in a blaze of gold, promising another sunny day tomorrow. It should have felt peaceful, but my mind was buzzing as I mentally sorted through everything I still needed to do.

First, find Florence and check who laid out the judges' table.

And now I had to tease out the story behind Liam's suspicious relief that Ronald Burrows was dead. Had be been seen around the stage?

They were all pieces of a puzzle that didn't fit quite together. Yet.

But with a little help from my grandmother's recipes, I was certain they would.

Chapter 12

THE EVENING AIR IN Briarvale carried a mix of fried onions, sugared doughnuts, and the unmistakable hum of anticipation, almost as if the village had decided, in defiance of tragedy, that celebration would continue, no matter the circumstances.

Twinkling fairy lights spread out from The Briar and Thorn, their soft glow stretching across the green like scattered stars, and laughter bubbled from every corner.

Although the murder of Ronald Burrows lingered in the backs of everyone's minds, it had already been tucked neatly into the edges of conversation, acknowledged, but not enough to spoil the festivities.

My gaze drifted to the judges' table, still cordoned off with police tape like a bizarre modern art installation. The fairy lights had been turned off in that area, as if everyone had chosen to ignore its presence. A rather portly police officer sat in the middle of the stage, one foot propped on a chair, while a younger woman officer patrolled round the perimeter, although she seemed more interested in watching the festival fun than in searching for clues.

"First time the Morris dancing shindig has had a police presence," Tom joked, his eyes following mine.

Inside The Briar and Thorn, the band was mid-sound check, their catchy guitar riffs weaving through the chatter while a singer tested her microphone with a voice that carried a perfect country heartbreak.

A group of men were standing in the doorway, drinks in hand. One of them broke away and hurried over.

"Tom!" he said. "The very person I need to talk to. My guttering is leaking something chronic. It's dripping right over my front door. Drowns me every time I walk outside. Think you can fix it?"

"Sure, Jim," said Tom, glancing at me with a pained expression. "I'll call round in the week and take a look."

"Great. How much do you think it will cost?" Jim carried on, oblivious to Tom's attempt to keep the conversation brief.

"Well, I'd need to see the extent of the damage first..." Tom tried again, taking a small step back toward me.

"Rough idea though?" Jim took a long swig of his beer, clearly settling in for a proper chat about the costs of home maintenance. "Things are so expensive these days. My neighbour paid a fortune for his roof repairs. Highway robbery, if you ask me."

Tom gave me his best get-me-out-of-here expression, but I could tell he was doomed to at least twenty more minutes of possible home improvement chat.

"You sort this out," I said with an understanding smile. "I'm going to mingle. See what village gossip I can dig up."

Tom's shoulders sagged in defeat as Jim launched into a detailed description of exactly where the water was pooling on his doorstep.

Leaving Tom, I scanned the scene, looking for someone who might unwittingly spill a useful clue about the murder.

There, rounding the corner from Briar Brook, was a woman.

A woman with chestnut hair.

Elegant. Striking.

The woman from my vision.

Her stride was quick, sharp, and every movement filled with tension. Even from a distance I could see it in her shoulders, the way her head twitched from side to side, watching, wary.

Her designer heels clicked against the pavement in an uneven staccato, as if her mind wasn't fully on where she was walking.

She powered past The HoneyPot, where Sylvia was clearing the last of the outside tables.

Sylvia spoke to her, but whatever she'd said, the woman waved it away, barely slowing as she veered towards The Briar and Thorn.

I hurried closer, but by the time I was at The HoneyPot, the woman had disappeared inside the pub through the side entrance.

Sylvia wiped her hands on a cloth and gave me a tired smile as I reached her.

"It's been a long day," she sighed. "The cafe's been non-stop. I thought I'd stay open until people drift off to listen to the band: make hay while the sun shines, you know?"

"Want me to help?" I offered.

"I wouldn't say no," Sylvia admitted, stacking cups neatly.

I began to gather plates off the tables, keeping my tone casual.

"That woman you spoke to a moment ago... Who was she?"

Sylvia glanced up. "You mean Vanessa?"

"Umm, thin woman, rather elegant looking," I clarified.

"Yeah, that's Vanessa Langley," said Sylvia in a not-so-impressed voice as we headed inside the tearoom with our stacks of crockery.

"Langley?" I gasped. "Is she Marcus Langley's wife?"

If the vision I'd had earlier came from Marcus, it would make sense he was looking at Vanessa.

But why did I get a vision from him?

Was Marcus our killer?

He'd had ample opportunity to put a poisoned envelope on the table next to Ronald.

But what was his motive?

Sylvia, focused on finishing up as quickly as possible, waved towards the counter.

"Leave the dishes there," she said. "I'm loading the dishwasher, then I'm done for tonight."

Mentally adding Marcus to my ever-growing list of murder suspects, I left Sylvia to her tidying and stepped back onto the street.

Tom was still trapped in conversation about leaky guttering, but across the green, Florence was on the move. She powered toward The Briar and Thorn, Eva's clipboard clutched tight, her usual nervous energy sharpened into something fiercer. Here was a woman determined to keep things running, even if it killed her.

If anyone knew what really happened with the judges' table, it was Florence. I needed to catch her before she disappeared into the next stage of her mission.

"Hi, Florence," I called, hurrying to fall into step beside her. "Any news on Eva?"

"Only that they're still questioning her," Florence offered, marching forward with the grim determination of a reluctant general rallying troops for a battle she never volunteered to fight.

It was clear she'd taken over the remaining festival duties in Eva's absence, and her expression was even more frazzled than usual.

I struggled to open the lid on the tin containing my goodies as we speed-walked across the grass. Loose-Tongue Toffee might be called for here.

"I've brought toffee," I said brightly. "Want a piece?"

Florence gave me a vague wave without slowing down. "Oh, no thank you. I haven't got time to stop."

"Try harder," chirped Einstein, trotting along beside us. "She's running on fumes and despair. She needs sugar... and magic."

"You need something to keep your energy up," I pressed, waving the tin under her nose. "A little pick-me-up never hurts."

That did the trick. She slowed, sniffing the air.

"Well, perhaps one," she conceded, pausing for a moment, selecting a toffee and popping it into her mouth.

"It must be a lot, stepping in for Eva," I said.

Florence sighed. "A mountain. I've had to take over all the announcements, check the band's here, make sure Marcus and Reverend Peters are ready to do their speeches, and double-check the raffle prizes. Do you know what?" She chewed the toffee thoughtfully. "Nobody appreciates how much organisation goes into a tombola. Nobody!"

"You're doing an amazing job," I said. "I mean, you even had the judges' table all set up earlier, right?"

Einstein purred approvingly. "Good angle," he said. "You're getting the hang of this questioning lark."

Florence shook her head. "Oh no, Eva does that all herself," she confirmed. "She always sets the table for the judges. Says it has to be 'just so'. Won't even let Percy help. He has to mind Charlie."

"Make that *very* good at questioning," Einstein said, the approval clear in his voice. "At this rate, we'll have the case solved before they draw the raffle."

I bit my lip. The trouble was, that little titbit certainly didn't help Eva's case.

"Mmm, this toffee is delicious," said Florence, licking a smudge of caramel from her finger.

"Thanks," I said. "So, did anyone else touch the judges' table? Before the competition started."

Florence frowned. "Umm, I suppose there were people milling about. It's hard to say. And I wasn't there all the time, I had to change for the dancing."

"How about Liam, from the Crimson Bells?" I suggested. "Did you see him?"

"Liam?" Florence swallowed the last of the toffee. "I don't think so... Oh!" She glanced at her watch. "I need to check the band are ready, and make absolutely certain Marcus hasn't wandered off to complain about the bunting again. And Reverend Peters is supposed to do the welcome speech. Unless he's still sulking about the raffle prize mix-up..."

She gave me a smile. "Thanks for the toffee." And she dashed off, clipboard clutched in her hand.

"I'm not even sure if that was enough time for the spell to kick in," I said to Einstein. "She might start confessing her darkest secrets to the lead guitarist."

Einstein stretched. "Better than nothing. What's our next move?"

I scanned the green. Somewhere in the sea of folk dancers and festival bunting, someone had to know the missing piece of the puzzle.

Preferably someone slower moving than Florence.

And that's when I spotted Percy Henshaw.

Chapter 13

I WAS SURPRISED TO see the station master here at all, considering his wife was currently being questioned by the police. He sat rigidly on a bench, his thin frame tense, as though held together by sheer willpower. His wire-rimmed glasses reflected the fairy lights, making his expression distant and unreadable. He was observing the festivities with the air of a man dutifully fulfilling an obligation rather than finding them entertaining.

Even little Charlie, perched on Percy's knee, looked subdued, his usual pint-sized bravado nowhere to be seen.

Einstein's tail swished confrontationally. "The Pocket Pooch doesn't look so brave without his dictator-in-chief," he commented. "I'll bet he won't so much as yap at me today."

"Aww, poor Charlie," I fixed Einstein with a hard stare. "Don't upset him."

"Who? Moi?" Einstein mewed innocently.

Ignoring him, I patted the small container inside my bag. "This'll be a proper test for the Truth-Whispering Muffins recipe."

Einstein was right about Charlie. He barely lifted his head as I slipped onto the bench beside Percy.

"Evening," I said lightly. "Big turnout tonight."

Percy turned, his expression softening.

"Oh, hello, Josie. Yes, the village always rallies for the Morris Dancing Festival. Tradition, you know."

Charlie's tail wagged half-heartedly, and I gave his soft, teddy-like head a gentle pat.

Einstein sighed dramatically.

"Ah, a rare moment of bonding," he drawled. "Make the most of it before he returns to his ankle-nipping ways."

I smothered a smile.

"I'm surprised to see you here, Percy," I ventured carefully.

He gave a resigned shrug.

"Eva insisted. Said a Henshaw should be present to represent the family, even if she wasn't able to be here herself." He adjusted his glasses. "Thirty-five years of marriage and I still can't win an argument with the woman."

The genuine affection in his voice surprised me, but Einstein chuckled.

"Smart man."

I ignored him.

"How's Eva doing?" I asked.

Percy exhaled.

"She is *furious*." He shook his head. "Not scared. More like outraged anyone would think she'd stoop to murder when she has so many more effective ways to deal with people who annoy her."

Einstein laughed again. "Like blacklisting their flower arrangements for eternity?" he muttered.

I ignored that, too, and reached into my bag for the tin of baking.

"Muffin?" I offered, trying to look as though I was casually sharing a snack and not conducting a covert magical interrogation.

Percy accepted without hesitation, taking a hungry bite, and I wondered whether he'd eaten anything at all since Eva's arrest.

"Excellent," he remarked, sounding mildly surprised. "I remember your grandmother was handy in the kitchen, too." He took another mouthful, larger this time. "Eva bakes muffins too, but they're not as tasty as this."

Einstein nudged my arm with his nose.

"The truth spell's kicking in fast. Keep him talking."

I gave a slight nod.

If Percy hadn't eaten for hours, the magic must be going straight into his bloodstream.

"You're certain Eva didn't kill Ronald?" I asked.

Percy sat back, the muffin nearly gone, the spell clearly working its charm.

"Absolutely," he said with conviction. "Eva likes to win, not eliminate the competition, even if that means bending the rules occasionally."

He hesitated, then, unexpectedly, he chuckled.

Charlie, his ears twitching at the change in Percy's mood, sat up.

"Truth be told," Percy continued, his own laughter seeming to surprise even himself, "Eva's not the only one who's sailed close to the wind when it comes to competitions."

I tried to imagine the prim stationmaster involved in anything remotely unscrupulous.

Einstein's ears perked up with interest. "Now that, my dear witch, is interesting news."

I raised an eyebrow. "You? Breaking rules? Percy Henshaw, I find that hard to believe."

Percy smirked. "It was the pub quiz a few years back. Eva was in charge of the questions, and I may have 'accidentally' fed my team a few answers ahead of time. Nothing serious. Merely the name of the third longest railway tunnel in Britain, and the exact date the 08:42 express from Polvarren first ran."

Charlie barked once, as if registering his owner's confession.

Percy sighed. "Eva accused me of cheating. She said she saw the gleam in my eye during the railway history round."

Einstein sniggered.

"A real rebel in disguise. I approve."

Percy patted Charlie's head. "Eva's a stickler for rules, but she doesn't kill people who annoy her. If she did, I wouldn't be here."

The affection in his voice was genuine. I smiled, heartened by the insight.

Trouble was, despite everything, Eva still looked guilty.

But if Marcus had tampered with the envelopes...

At that moment, a shadow fell across us. I looked up to see Edwin Fletcher, the village shopkeeper. Einstein immediately pretended not to notice him, which was generous considering Edwin had evicted him from the shop on more than one occasion, brandishing a broom like an exorcist and muttering about fur and food safety.

"Evening, Josie," Edwin said, his voice warm as ever. "And Percy. How are you holding up?"

"As well as can be expected," Percy replied, which I assumed was man-code for my-wife-is-being-interrogated-for-murder-and-I'm-stress-cuddling-the-dog.

Edwin nodded sympathetically, his gaze falling on the black tin in my lap. "Ah, you've brought your famous baking. Liam was raving about it earlier. He was singing his praises about Briarwood Gables too. Looks like your B&B venture's a winner."

He peered at the Memory-Sparking Shortbread with undisguised interest.

"Would you like to see what all the fuss is about?" I asked, holding out the tub.

Edwin's eyes lit up with anticipation. "Well, it would be rude to refuse," he replied. "I've always had a sweet tooth. Comes with growing up above a shop full of temptations."

His fingers hovered momentarily before choosing a slice that had been cut larger than the others.

I grinned. If there was even a whiff of scandal in the village, Edwin Fletcher would have sniffed it out before breakfast. He was a great person to talk to.

"Oh! Lovely bit of shortbread, Josie," Edwin said, licking a stray crumb from his finger. "You should sell these in the shop, you know. We'll be rich by Christmas."

"If you don't chase the customers away with a broom," Einstein muttered.

"I'll think about it, Edwin," I replied, waiting for the enchantment to work its magic.

"You know," said Edwin, taking another bite, chewing thoughtfully, "this takes me back to the year of the Great Biscuit Scandal."

"Oh, I remember that fiasco," put in Percy.

"What happened?" I asked.

"Old Mr Thatcher, the captain of the Whirligig Wobblers back then, used to stand right by the judges' table, jotting down every word they said about other teams."

A slight furrow appeared between his brows, the expression you get when a thought slips past and you're scrambling to reel it in.

"He claimed it was for 'strategy'. Turned out he was pocketing the biscuits meant for the officials." Edwin chuckled, shaking his head at the remembered mischief. "They caught him with his pockets full of Jammie Dodgers during the final judging."

"No!"

"Oh yes. Banned him from the judges' table for three whole years."

This information, while entertaining, wasn't getting me any closer to solving the case.

"I can't believe everyone takes the competition so seriously," I ventured. "I mean, Eva was so theatrical about announcing the winners, and making sure all the scorecards and envelopes were perfectly aligned."

Percy barked out a laugh that sent a nearby pigeon flapping for the trees. "She'd rather buy a brand new packet of envelopes than have one that didn't match the others," he chortled.

Einstein twisted through my legs. "Another nice line of questioning," he said approvingly.

"You're right about the envelopes," Edwin agreed. "The latest batch I ordered to sell were a slightly different size from last year's. Eva *did* buy a whole new set rather than have an odd one."

I smiled politely, filing that information away.

Edwin rubbed his chin, his brow furrowing. "And then Mrs Langley came in for an envelope last night," he went on, his tone shifting. "She made almost as much fuss."

"Vanessa Langley," I blurted out.

Now that was interesting.

"What kind of fuss?" I asked.

Edwin let out a dry chuckle. "Well, she was proper particular. Said she had something important to seal up." He gestured vaguely. "But she didn't grab any old envelope off the shelf. Oh no, she wanted the exact same ones as Eva bought."

Einstein stood still by my feet, clearly intrigued. "Suspiciously picky," he murmured, his eyes gleaming.

Edwin continued. "I told her I had plenty of other envelopes, fancier ones, even, but she wasn't interested. Said, and I quote, 'If it's good enough for Eva Henshaw, it's good enough for me'."

"What did she want it for?" I asked.

Edwin shrugged. "She didn't say. Paid for it quickly and left. Walked out without so much as waiting for her receipt."

Einstein flicked his tail in satisfaction. "Well, she wasn't exactly going to admit she needed it to murder Ronald Burrows, now was she?"

Chapter 14

E DWIN, HOWEVER, WAS ONLY getting started.

"Actually, come to think of it," he said, brushing crumbs from his jumper, "I spotted Nigel, you know, the sandy-haired lad from the Springleaf Ramblers, snooping round the judges' table before they announced the winners."

He leaned forward, his brows knitting together thoughtfully.

"He looked proper shifty, he did. Glancing around like he'd lost a puppy... or a conscience. Reminded me of old Mr Thatcher and the Great Biscuit Scandal."

Einstein sighed. "Not another plot twist."

I frowned. "Nigel from the Ramblers?" I said, remembering the cold-hearted conversation I'd overheard from that team when Ronald had first collapsed.

Edwin nodded solemnly. "Mmm. Looked like he wanted a peek at the results. Or maybe he fancied helping himself to a biscuit."

"Or he was slipping in a poisoned envelope for Ronald Burrows," purred Einstein.

Percy appeared to consider this. "Are you talking about Nigel Grimsby? The one who works at the garden centre? He doesn't seem the type for skulduggery."

"That's the one," Edwin confirmed. "Sandy hair, always looks like he's been blown in by a strong wind. Nice enough lad. Has a taste for Jaffa Cakes. Buys them from the shop in bulk."

Einstein chuckled. "That definitely makes him a murderer."

"Mind you, he might be totally innocent," said Edwin. "Probably is. I'm simply saying it looked odd."

I nodded. If Nigel had been near the judges' table before Ronald collapsed, he might have seen something important, even if he wasn't involved himself. Now I needed to talk to him as well.

Edwin brushed the last shortbread crumbs from his hands.

"Enough sitting here. I need something warming after all this talk of judges and tables. The drinks van serves a mean cup of hot chocolate. They put cream and marshmallows in." He turned to Percy. "What do you say?"

Percy checked his watch, a deeply ingrained reflex that suggested he usually timed his tea breaks with a stopwatch.

But there was nothing usual about tonight.

He plonked Charlie on the ground.

"Why not?" he said.

Edwin looked at me. "You coming, Josie?"

I shook my head.

"I'll catch up with you later," I said, gathering my container of baked goods. "There's someone I want to speak to first."

As Edwin, Percy and Charlie headed for the hot drinks stall, their figures silhouetted against the warm glow of the festival lights, my eyes searched the groups milling on the green.

The after-contest celebrations were in full swing, with clusters of people gathered around the various stalls. The air was alive with laughter, snatches of music, and the occasional cheer from children, wild-eyed on sugar and the thrill of staying up late, as they wove a wobbly conga line round the ice-cream van.

But I couldn't see any of the suspects I needed to speak to, and I was getting rather behind in my interrogations.

I still hadn't found out about Liam and his grudge against Ronald.

I had no idea why Vanessa and Marcus would want to kill his fellow judge.

And now there was Nigel, from the Springleaf Ramblers, to complicate matters.

Everyone I spoke to seemed to tangle the mystery further, rather than help solve it.

I looked towards The Briar and Thorn. Its windows glowed with warm light, the sound of music and conversation spilling out into the night.

If I were a Morris dancer who'd been performing this afternoon, that's where I'd likely be.

I straightened my shoulders, adjusted my tin of enchanted snacks, and headed for the door, ready to find the next piece of the puzzle.

Einstein slowed as we approached the entrance, eyeing the pub as if it were a pit of chaos involving beer fumes and human noise and I was planning to drag him in by the nose.

"I'm not convinced about this, Josie," he murmured, his tail flicking sharply. "I'm a cat of refinement."

I shrugged. "Stay outside, if you want."

Einstein sniffed. "What, and miss all the sleuthing?"

"Well, don't complain then."

But the moment we stepped inside, Einstein's ears flattened at the sudden roar of laughter and music, weaving closer to my legs as if to shield himself from the sheer disorder of it all, and I have to admit it was overwhelming for me too.

"Too many humans, too much shouting, and a nasty sticky floor," Einstein sniffed. "This establishment is not designed for creatures of my breeding."

I ignored him, scanning the crowd for Nigel, Marcus or Vanessa, but Einstein continued his low-key protest.

"If I get trodden on," Einstein huffed, "I'm suing."

I'd never been into The Briar and Thorn in all the weeks since I'd arrived in Briarvale. I'm not a big drinker, and I'm probably showing my age here, but after spending my days patching up ancient plumbing, coaxing antique furniture back to life, and trying not to throttle my talking cat, I was far more inclined towards a book and an early night than a trip to the pub.

But I knew Pippa Mayhew, the landlady. We'd chatted often enough while she watered the hanging baskets overflowing with bright flowers outside the pub, or wrangled barrels of beer into the cellar with the strength of someone twice her size.

She reminded me of Kim, my daughter, being about the same age, with the same no-nonsense energy and bubbly enthusiasm for life.

Now, stepping inside the pub for the first time, I was immediately swallowed by the warm chaos of it all.

The Briar and Thorn was everything a proper village pub should be: low, beamed ceilings, scuffed wooden floors, a fireplace in the far corner, and a bar that looked like it had stories soaked into the grain. The scent of hops, spilled cider, and something deep-fried lingered in the air, mingling with laughter and the thrum of live folk music tuning up in the background.

It was cosy, chaotic and packed wall-to-wall with post-festival cheer.

And it was also the last place you'd expect anyone to be playing magical detective armed with a tin of enchanted baked goods.

I couldn't see Liam, Marcus or Vanessa, and, as the Springleaf Ramblers would have changed out of their Morris dancing costumes by now, the only way to identify Nigel was through Edwin's description of his wild, sandy hair.

I stood on tiptoe, scanning the crowd with increasing frustration.

This was getting me nowhere.

"Josie!" a voice bellowed.

Liam cut through the mass of bodies, striding towards me like he was still wielding his Morris stick in full swing.

Behind him were two of his team-mates, Connor and Dylan, whom I recognised from Briarwood Gables. They had the remains of the war-paint they'd worn for the contest still smudged across their faces.

"I told them about that toffee of yours," Liam said, pointing a finger at me like I was a celebrity chef. "If breakfast's half as good, we're in for a treat."

I winced, silently thanking the stars (and Sylvia from The HoneyPot) that I'd enlisted Paula, one of the cooks from the tearoom, to help me in the morning. Magical baking was one thing, but turning out a full English breakfast for a house full of guests? That required a whole other set of skills, and before I came to Briarvale, my culinary legacy had mostly involved burnt toast and takeaway menus.

Dylan peered at the tin I was carrying.

"Is that what I think it is?" he asked, his eyes lighting up. "Liam said your toffee tastes better than his mum's, which might get him written out of her will."

Liam had spotted the container of goodies, too. His eyes widened greedily. "Oh! You brought some? You have to let these idiots try something, Josie."

Before I had a chance to protest, Liam had nudged me to a recently vacated table.

"Really, my cooking is nothing special," I tried to demur, suddenly anxious about sharing my enchanted bakes with this enthusiastic audience.

But then, what better moment to dig into the 'grudges and debts' against Ronald Burrows that Liam had hinted at?

Chapter 15

F ORGETTING ABOUT NIGEL FOR the time being, I sat down, placing the tin on the table in front of me.

"Josie's being modest," Liam declared. "And after today's completely botched decision from the judges, we all need something sweet to take the edge off."

I opened the container with the hesitation of a bomb disposal expert, and Liam and his friends swooped in like vultures, each grabbing whatever appealed to them most, oblivious to the fact they were consuming highly specific enchantments.

Einstein's ears went flat.

"You need to keep control of this, Josie," he muttered. "Or are we conducting a social experiment in magical side-effects?"

As if to make his point, Pippa bustled past, a tray of empty glasses balanced expertly on one hand. She paused, eyeing the open tin with amused suspicion.

"Are you bringing your own catering now?" she asked, mock-serious.

"Well, I..." I started, but Pippa nabbed a Truth-Whispering Muffin before I had chance stop her.

Einstein gave me an exasperated look. "You do realise this is how spell-infused chaos begins," he chuntered. "First a muffin, then an accidental confession, then a village-wide scandal!"

He was right. This was spiralling out of control. I certainly didn't want my enchanted treats being consumed at random by half the village in a frenzied magical bake sale free-for-all. The Briar and Thorn was in danger of becoming an impromptu magical confessional.

I snapped the lid shut as Pippa flashed me a quick smile of appreciation before she vanished into the crowd, leaving behind only the sound of Liam's mates squabbling over the biggest slice of Memory-Sparking Shortbread.

Connor took a bite and chewed his shortbread thoughtfully.

"You know," he said, voice soft with nostalgia, "these remind me of being twelve. Me and Liam were round at Dyl's house. Thick as thieves we were back then."

"Still are," added Dylan.

Connor grinned. "Dyl's mum and dad were into the Morris dancing and they needed extras," he continued. "Well, his mum came to talk to us this day, offering cookies, and before we knew it, she'd roped us into the troupe."

Dylan chuckled. "Mum thought giving twelve-year-old boys sticks and permission to whack each other would be a great bonding experience."

Liam flashed me a perfect smile. "That's how I lost my front tooth." He tapped it lightly with his finger. "This one's false, you know."

"I'd never have guessed," I said politely, trying to think how to get round to the real reason I was sitting here. "No wonder you're so good, if you've been dancing since you were twelve," I ventured. "You must've been winning competitions for years."

Dylan nodded enthusiastically, still munching his shortbread.

"The year we turned sixteen," he told me, "we won every contest... except one."

Connor groaned. "Yeah, the one Liam bet Ronald Burrows we'd win."

That got my attention.

"Wasn't it a bit silly to bet with the judge?" I asked.

Liam sat straighter, his expression darkening. "Oh, Burrows wasn't a judge back then," he said defensively.

He was only halfway through his shortbread, but I could see the memory was crystal-clear to him.

"Ronald's wife was in the Wobblers," Liam explained, "and he coached them. She'd only been dancing for two years, but the idiot acted like he was a world-class expert."

Connor snorted. "Which he must have been, because that was the only year the Wobblers ever got on the scoreboard."

Liam scowled. "Yeah, but what kind of a man bets a sixteen-year-old two hundred pounds?" he growled. "And Burrows insisted I paid every penny. Took me a whole year to earn it."

"Never mind, mate," said Dylan, clapping Liam round the shoulders cheerfully. "He's gone now. He'll never be able to taunt you with it again."

Was that too cheerful?

Did that make Dylan a suspect too?

Connor dusted off the last crumbs of his shortbread.

"I don't like to speak ill of the dead," he said, "but Burrows did have a nasty habit of mentioning the bet at every opportunity. Called him 'Twinkletoes the Debtor'."

His tone grew hard.

"He wasn't a good guy, and he certainly knew how to hold a grudge. There was one judge this afternoon who didn't even put us in the top three, and I'd bet my bells it was Ronald. I'm glad he's out of the way. Here's hoping we can start winning again now."

And my mind flipped back to The HoneyPot when Ronald had commented about Liam 'dancing for his dinner'. Burrows had certainly known how to rub salt in an old wound. No wonder Liam and the others didn't like him.

That bumped Liam up in the 'motive' stakes. And I mentally added Daryl to my suspect list, too. Both of them definitely had their reasons, but did either have the opportunity?

Liam stood up abruptly.

"I'm going to get another round in," he announced. Then without warning he casually popped the lid off my baking tin and helped himself to another piece of toffee, like it was part of the drinks order.

Einstein let out a pained yowl. "Yikes! That's his third piece. Let's hope enough time has passed since the first two that he won't start speaking in rhyme."

I snatched the tin onto my knee and snapped the lid shut forcefully.

Pippa dropped into the empty chair beside to me with the dramatic sigh of a person who'd been on their feet for fourteen hours straight.

I braced myself for whatever truth-whispering side-effects might come next.

"Oh, my word," she groaned, kicking one shoe off underneath the table. "It's been festival madness in here all day. But I have to tell you, Josie. Your muffins? Glorious."

"I'm glad you like them." I paused a moment. "Hey, I don't suppose you've seen Nigel, from the Springfield Ramblers?" I asked.

Pippa pursed her lips. "Sandy hair? Looks like he's been through a hedge on a bike?"

"That's him."

She twisted round. "Well, he was by the dartboard, chatting up one of the Merry Maids, but they're not there now." She winked at me. "This is my pub. I see everything, you know?"

"What about Vanessa and Marcus Langley?" I asked.

Pippa rolled her eyes. "Don't remind me about those two," she sighed. "They usually stay at some fancy hotel in St Austell, but there was a mix-up and it was booked out, so they've been 'roughing it' here in the one room we have that wasn't affected by our great plumbing apocalypse."

I thought about that. That explained why I'd seen Vanessa going in through the side door.

"But being our only guests has given them the run of the place," Pippa groaned. "They want breakfast service, silly requests, the royal treatment. And let me tell you, they are *hard* work."

She leaned across the table towards me.

"Vanessa is the queen of high maintenance. Asked for hand-churned butter served on antique china this morning." A mischievous grin spread over Pippa's face. "I gave her margarine on a saucer I bought from the supermarket. She didn't seem to notice the difference."

We both dissolved into giggles, and I filed that tip away for similar picky guests I might encounter at Briarwood Gables.

"Umm, have you noticed anything... strange about them?" I asked.

"Well..." Pippa started.

But at that moment, a loud crash and the sound of breaking glass echoed from the bar.

"Uh oh! That sounds bad." She hastily reclaimed her shoe from beneath the table. "I'll tell you about Vanessa later. No rest for the wicked, eh?"

Einstein's whiskers twitched with irritation. "Right when we were getting to the interesting part," he grumbled.

I was about to stand up, but then Liam returned to the table, a tray of drinks balanced precariously in his hands. His smile was wide, and his eyebrows dramatically arched as if he was an actor about to deliver his opening lines.

"Thirsty lads and ladies fair," he boomed theatrically, "your liquid joy is waiting there!"

"Wait? What?" said Connor, staring at Liam. "Are you rhyming?"

Dylan burst out laughing. "Liams's gone full Shakespeare. Is this your new party trick, mate?"

Einstein covered his face with a paw. "That third toffee has taken effect. Don't say I didn't warn you."

"What can I do?" I mouthed.

Einstein shrugged. "Only wait it out," he said, confirming my worst fears. "It'll pass eventually."

Liam bowed dramatically and swept an imaginary hat from his head.

"A tipple here, a toast begun,

To friends, and fun, and setting suns.

And while I've got this bard-like knack,

I beg you all, don't give me flak!"

Connor practically fell off his chair laughing. "Oh, this is the best thing that's happened all festival."

Liam, looking confused, handed Connor his pint, declaring,

"Ales for all and none shall pout,

Drink it in, your spirits shout!"

He rubbed his temple.

"Why can't I stop this weird old verse,

It's like my brain's been... cursed,

By... worse."

Einstein groaned loudly. "Josie, we need a safety protocol for excessive magical snacking." He flicked his tail. "Next time, slap a warning on the tin. Something subtle, like: 'May cause spontaneous poetry'."

"I'll start printing labels," I muttered.

Liam had taken to rhyming the drinks menu, when a sharp screech from the pub's PA system interrupted his flow.

Florence stood on the tiny stage. She was gripping Eva's clipboard in one hand, the microphone in the other.

"Ladies and gentlemen," she announced, her voice trembling, but still strong. "Please welcome our band for the evening... the toe-tapping Bodmin Barn Owls!"

A wave of applause went up as a group of musicians shuffled onto the stage, carrying fiddles and guitars, and fronted by a singer with a gloriously glittery tambourine.

Liam raised his glass.

"To music now, and dancing soon,

Just don't request a late-night tune."

Dylan snorted beer through his nose. "Mate, you're hilarious tonight."

Liam took a long sip of his pint and launched into a rhyme about banjos and bar snacks.

"Oh, for the love of jam doughnuts," Einstein muttered. "He's getting worse."

I stood up, retrieving my container of chaos from under the table.

I wasn't going to get any more sense out of Liam. It was time I found someone else to interview.

Chapter 16

T HE MUSIC HAD PICKED up in The Briar and Thorn, and singing and laughter rose with it, carried on the warm scent of good ale.

The dartboard corner was now being monopolised by two families arguing over which dad had the worst aim, and the Merry Maid whom Pippa had noticed chatting up Nigel earlier was batting her eyelashes at a bald guy, who was clearly not him.

At the bar, Pippa was still busy sweeping up shards of the broken beer glasses with tired resignation. There was no chance to speak to her without getting in the way of her clean-up efforts, which would be mean. Whatever odd thing she'd noticed about the Langleys, other than the fact that they were super-demanding house guests, would have to wait for later.

I manoeuvred through the crowd toward the door.

Einstein trailed behind me, weaving between drinkers' legs. He was lifting his paws with feline distaste, as if each step was a personal insult.

As soon as we stepped outside, he exhaled dramatically, giving his fur an exaggerated shake, as though cleansing himself of the sticky, beer-slicked floor trauma.

"Finally, fresh air. I was moments away from sacrificing my dignity and requesting to be carried out."

He flicked his tail, eyes sharp.

"So? Where to next? I hope it's somewhere with less beer, and a bit more discretion with enchanted pastries."

"I need to speak to Nigel and Marcus and Vanessa," I told him. "It would be good to eliminate suspects instead of accumulating them."

Einstein gave a purr of agreement.

The crowd on the green had thinned, drawn indoors by the jaunty riffs of the Bodmin Barn Owls. Only a few small clusters of people remained, gathered around the food vans, while several members of the Black Boars, drunk beyond all doubt, attempted an impromptu recreation of their competition performance under the old tree in the middle.

Sitting apart on a low stone wall, I caught sight of Tom. Murphy was curled at his feet, his black and white coat silvered in the moonlight.

Tom was gazing up at the stars, a bottle of elderflower cordial resting by his side.

Murphy spotted us and bounded over, his tail wagging enthusiastically. I scruffed behind his ears as I settled on the wall beside them.

"Too noisy for Murphy in there," Tom told me. "And honestly? Too noisy for me."

"Same," I agreed.

Einstein stretched, swishing his tail with lingering disdain.

"A racket like that should be classified as a crime. Sticky floors, shouting humans, and no regard for feline dignity."

He glanced toward Murphy, giving a curt nod.

"For once, I agree with the dog."

I turned to Tom. "Did you sort out a time to check Jim's guttering?"

He huffed a quiet breath, shaking his head. "Yeah, first thing Monday," he said. "Though it would've been nice to make it ten steps into the festival before being ambushed about it."

I cringed, knowing full well Jim had cornered him and that I'd slipped away, leaving him to handle the conversation alone, in favour of my investigations.

I shot him a sideways glance.

Was he annoyed I'd done that? He didn't look angry.

Gary would have been furious.

I gave him a sheepish smile, then nodded toward the bottle on the wall.

"Cordial?"

He followed my gaze and gave a small, crooked smile. "Haven't touched alcohol in years. Not since..." He trailed off. "Well, not since my life went... a bit sideways."

I glanced at him. He had that faraway look I caught sometimes.

"After your wife?" I asked gently.

He nodded, still gazing at the sky.

"When Lucy died... it took me a long time to climb out of that hole. If it hadn't been for your grandmother..." He twisted the bottle cap, his gaze distant. "She gave me work when no one else would. Gave me something to fix that wasn't myself." He paused, still holding the bottle. "I still wake up sometimes expecting Lucy to be next to me. And then I feel guilty that I'm here, and she's not."

I bit my lip. "I still wake up expecting to find Gary in my bed," I admitted.

I thought about the divorce papers sitting on the hall table, waiting for my signature.

"Only *I'm* not sorry that he's not."

The words hung in the air, the silence saying more than I ever could.

Over in the pub, the music was muffled to a bearable thump beneath the quiet of the night.

"You're allowed to start again, you know," I said quietly.

Tom looked at me then. I mean, *really* looked.

"Maybe," he said. "But baggage like mine doesn't exactly make me desirable property."

I laughed softly. "Oh, I don't know. You've got a decent view, solid foundations..."

Tom chuckled, shaking his head. "And a roof in desperate need of repairs."

"We all have our leaks," I said with a smile.

We sat there a moment longer. Tom took a sip of his cordial, the bottle making a soft clink against the stone wall. "So..." he asked, his voice lighter now. "How's the sleuthing?"

He wasn't teasing, just asking. I appreciated that.

I exhaled, long and slow. "Frustrating. I've collected enough village gossip to write a column for the *Polvarren Herald*, but none of it's giving me what I need. And I can't find Nigel from the Springleaf Ramblers. I don't even truly know what he looks like out of costume."

Tom straightened, his expression brightening. "Nigel?" he exclaimed. "Sandy-haired lad, works at the garden centre?"

My pulse quickened. "That's him. Edwin Fletcher mentioned seeing him near the judges' table before the murder happened."

Tom nodded, catching on immediately.

"Might be important. And I saw Nigel not ten minutes ago chatting up the girl in the burger van. Want me to get him for you? He helped me build the chicken coop. Good lad, bit of a chatterbox, but handy with a hammer."

"That would be brilliant."

Tom gave me a reassuring smile. "Keep an eye on Murphy. I'll be right back."

And off he went across the green with a deliberate stride.

Behind me, Einstein let out a theatrical sigh.

"Oh, that's rich," he muttered. "I endure sticky floors, questionable company, and an assault on my refined sensibilities, and now it's all, 'Oooh, Tom, go fetch Nigel'. No appreciation for your furry workforce."

I glanced down at him, amused. "Have you remembered where you smelled that other scent in the results box yet?"

"No."

"Then less sulking, more sleuthing."

Einstein grumbled something under his breath that sounded something like "glorified bloodhound", but he didn't argue further.

As I watched Tom powering over the green, a familiar figure stepped out of The Briar and Thorn, her expression tired but happy.

Sylvia.

I gave her a wave. "I thought you'd be at home with your feet up by now."

Sylvia returned a weary smile. "I couldn't leave without saying goodbye to Liam and the lads from the Bells," she said, her tone full of fond affection. "Such lovely boys. Although, I'm afraid Liam might have had one cider too many. He's talking in silly rhymes." She rolled her eyes. "You know what he said to me?"

I groaned. "Go on."

"It was along the lines of, 'Sylvia's cooking is truly divine, See you next year. Same food, same time'!"

Einstein flicked a dismissive paw. "His rhymes are not getting any better."

A thought struck me, sharp enough to make me stand up so fast that Einstein jumped off the wall in surprise.

"Wait! Did the Crimson Bells dance outside The HoneyPot right up until the contest began?"

Sylvia nodded without hesitation.

"And none of them left?" I pressed. "Liam, Daryl... They were there the whole time?"

She frowned, as if confused by my doubt.

"Oh, one hundred percent," she assured me. "The whole team was there. I kept nipping outside to catch their routines whenever I had a moment. In fact..."

She pulled out her phone, tapping the screen.

"I took some videos of them. See? I put it on their website. It helps them get recognised. And it helps me too because people see The HoneyPot."

I grinned, a wave of relief settling in.

If Liam and the others were outside The HoneyPot the entire time until the contest began, there was no way they could have swapped out the poisoned envelope on the judges' table.

And I was pleased about that. Sylvia was right: the Crimson Bells *were* nice lads.

Einstein gave a dramatic stretch, clearly unimpressed with my moment of satisfaction.

"Wonderful. You're thrilled Liam *isn't* a murderer. Do let me know when you've eliminated the rest of the human race."

I rolled my eyes, but the relief lingered anyway.

Sylvia exhaled, shifting her bag onto her shoulder. "Right," she said. "That's me done. Time I headed home."

A few minutes later, Tom returned with a whirlwind of enthusiasm in the shape of Nigel Grimsby.

Sandy hair. Slightly wild expression. Chattering fast enough to power a wind turbine.

"...and then the ornamental gnome exploded. Right into the compost! My manager said it was a disaster zone. You'd think I'd burned down the entire garden centre."

I grinned.

Nigel might be the killer, but even if he wasn't, he had the air of someone likely to witness something crucial and not think twice about it.

I took a steadying breath, crossing my fingers that I was right.

"Now," I whispered to Einstein, "let's see if Nigel has any answers."

Chapter 17

"Hey, Josie," Tom said as they reached us, Murphy circling once before returning to Tom's side. "This is Nigel Grimsby. Nigel, Josie Appleton."

"Brilliant to meet you," Nigel exclaimed, extending a hand. His grip was firm and friendly, his smile genuine beneath a mop of sandy-blond hair that did indeed look like he'd blown in on the east wind.

"I've driven past Briarwood Gables loads of times delivering plants for the garden centre," Nigel chatted. "Your driveway always looks so inviting, and the trees are magnificent."

"Thanks," I said. "But that's all down to Tom."

Tom waved away the praise, then he rubbed his hand over his face like Nigel's chatter had already given him earache.

"I'm going to get a hot drink," he said, gesturing towards a nearby van. "Want anything?"

"I wouldn't mind a coffee," Nigel shot in cheekily.

Tom snorted, shaking his head. "I wasn't asking you." Then he let out a sigh in mock resignation. "Fine," he said. "What kind?"

"Latte," Nigel grinned, throwing in a mischievous wink as Tom headed off with Murphy trotting beside him.

"Tom said I should come and meet you, to try some of your baking," Nigel continued, words tumbling out so fast I don't know when he had time for breath. "And the Crimson Bells couldn't stop raving about it earlier." He grinned. "You've got quite the reputation."

I looked down at my grandmother's tin containing the enchanted treats, considering which would be most useful.

Loose-Tongue Toffee? Nigel-the-Chatterbox didn't need any of that.

Memory-Sparking Shortbread might help him recall details he hadn't thought relevant.

But the Truth-Whispering Muffins would encourage Nigel to be honest about what he'd been doing at the judges' table. That seemed my best bet.

Nigel's eyes widened as I lifted the lid, his excitement far too eager for my liking.

"I recommend the muffins," I told him.

"Whoa, these look incredible!" Nigel reached forward with the excitement of a child spotting free sweets at a market stall.

I shifted the tin back, holding it out of reach.

"One," I said firmly. "Take only one."

Nigel batted his eyelashes at me. "Oh, but how am I supposed to judge your baking if I don't try each kind? My mum always says you learn a lot about a baker by sampling the full spread. Tests their range, you know?"

Einstein darted forward, positioning himself between Nigel's eager hands and the bakes with the selfless loyalty of a furry bodyguard.

"And Mum's right," Nigel went on. "A baker's skill is tested by variety. A single treat? Not a fair assessment."

I tilted the tin away again.

"One. No exceptions. There are other people who want to try them."

Nigel grinned, far too charming. "Of course, I understand."

He reached in, choosing the Truth-Whispering Muffin, and I let out a sigh of relief, until I realised he was also swiping a small piece of shortbread.

Einstein reacted first, pawing at Nigel's sleeve as I lunged to block his hand.

"Oi! No pastry pilfering!" I snapped.

But Nigel, faster than either I or Einstein expected, and far too nimble for someone who claimed to struggle with Morris dancing footwork, flashed a grin and spun away. The piece of Loose-Tongue Toffee he'd taken was already wedged between his teeth.

"Now this is a proper tasting session," he chortled, somehow managing to get all three magical bakes into his mouth at the same time.

Einstein hissed in exasperation.

"You let him eat them all!" he yowled. "Do something?"

I snatched Einstein off the ground. "What do you suggest?" I muttered into his fur.

Einstein rubbed his face against mine in an uncharacteristic show of affection. "Oh, you want to pick my brains, eh? And here I was thinking we were having a bonding moment."

"Be serious," I chided.

Einstein patted my face with his paw. "You could always try sticking your fingers down his throat and see if you can get him to throw the magic back up?"

I stared at him, appalled. "That is disgusting."

"You asked for my advice," said Einstein. "I'm being practical."

"But it's not going to happen."

I looked at Nigel, his cheeks doing an impression of a greedy chipmunk as he munched away.

"What happens now that he's eaten three spells?"

"I don't remember any of my witches trying it," said Einstein.

I felt a flutter of panic.

"Oh dear," I murmured, setting Einstein back down on the ground.

"Oh dear, indeed," he replied, his eyes following Nigel as he swallowed the last morsel of muffin.

Nigel beamed at us, oblivious to the magical disaster that was brewing.

"You've got a cool cat," he declared, crumbs catching in the corners of his smile. "And your baking is brilliant. It's so light! What's your secret?"

"They're my grandmother's recipes," I said, watching him nervously.

"These have fantastic texture," he murmured, licking his thumb. "The muffins are incredible, and the shortbread? My gran used to make it, but it always turned out a bit hard. You had to dunk it in your tea. Yours melts on the tongue, and I swear, there's something about it that makes me remember childhood Christmases. Once, when I was eight, I climbed up on the wardrobe in my parent's room to peek at my presents..."

His voice trailed off, his eyes taking on that unfocused glaze I'd seen in the others when the magic was working. But Nigel was different. A sort of shimmering quality, as the three enchantments began layering over each other.

"I got a bike," he blurted out.

"Pardon?"

"For Christmas," he clarified. "It was blue. I loved that bike."

Einstein flicked his tail against my ankle.

"I'd get your questioning in fast," he suggested. "Before he narrates his entire childhood."

I nodded.

"Hey, Nigel!" I called. "You were at the judging table this afternoon. What were you up to?"

Einstein made a noise like he was coughing up a hairball. "Well, you weren't beating about the bush with that one."

"Ah, yes." Nigel spread his arms wide. "The esteemed judges' table. The place where Morris dancing dreams go to die."

His words poured out fast, the enchantments gripping him with full force now.

"I wasn't trying to cheat. I was... information gathering!"

He shook his head, looking embarrassed.

"Not my proudest moment, but it was a strategic approach. The Ramblers have never placed above third, you see, and I thought, what if the judges always mark us down for the same things? What if there's some secret technique we're missing? So I hopped onto the stage, trying to sneak a peek at their notes."

Einstein gave a sigh. "So, he wasn't planting envelopes laced with cyanide then. Pity."

"Which reminds me," continued Nigel, without pausing for breath, "I tried to cheat on a spelling test in Year Four. Total disaster. I wrote the answers on the inside of my wrist, but I got sweaty, and they smudged. Ended up spelling 'necessary' as 'necces-sorry,' which summed up my entire day after the teacher saw the writing on my hands."

"Yes, but what about the judging table?" I insisted.

"Right! Right. The table. So, I was leaning in, and I managed to make out a few remarks. 'Timing inconsistent.' 'Footwork sloppy.' 'Not enough elevation on the jumps', which is unfair because have they tried to jump in those shoes?"

"Definitely unfair," I agreed. "Anything else? Did you touch the envelopes?"

"No, but Marcus Langley did! He's the posh judge with the fancy watch worth more than my car. He was straightening them like his life depended on it."

I leaned forward. "So, Marcus touched the envelopes?"

Nigel gave a sharp nod.

"He did. Made them all neat."

His eyes glazed over. "Speaking of neatness, I tried to tame my hair before the last works' Christmas party. Spent two hours sculpting it into something presentable. Walked outside, and the first gust of wind turned me into a human dandelion."

"Human dandelion!" Einstein chortled. "In his present state, I suspect a passing breeze might scatter the poor lad across the village."

I rubbed my forehead. "Was there anyone else at the judges' table? Someone who shouldn't have been there?"

Nigel tapped the side of his nose. "Now you mention it, when I was looking at the notes, there was an ant was carrying another bug, like five times its size." He shook his head. "Ants shouldn't be on the table, but that was some super-strong beast."

And then he launched into an in-depth analysis of Morris dancing bell patterns, his speech speeding up, his gestures growing wilder. A sheen of sweat was forming on his forehead.

Einstein circled round my ankles, his fur bristling with concern. "I think we may have a problem," he murmured. "Dilated pupils, excessive speech, slight tremor in his limbs. He's in magical overload. He'll be seeing auras trailing behind everyone next and having an irrational craving for pickled foods."

Nigel paused mid-sentence to stare with fascination at my hands.

"Your fingers are glowing blue," he informed me, his voice serious. "And you don't happen to have any pickled onions in that box of yours, do you? I really fancy some. Strange, I never liked them before."

Guilt settled in my stomach.

"We should get you home, Nigel," I suggested. "It's been a long day."

Nigel nodded, his movements becoming more and more exaggerated. "Yes, home. Although you're such a nice person, Josie, I feel I can tell you anything. Like how I dyed all my mother's white laundry pink, or how I'm terrified of geese, or how Vanessa Langley was arguing with Daryl earlier."

That got my attention. "Vanessa and Daryl?"

"Yeah, they were standing by the bridge over the stream, and she was furious about something," Nigel told me. "Jabbing her finger into his chest, and he looked all flustered, which is not like him, especially around a woman." He leaned closer. "I think Daryl bribes the judges. I think that's how the Green Stags always win."

My heart beat faster.

I was one hundred percent certain Nigel's reason for being up on the stage with the judges was the truth. And if Daryl was bribing Marcus...

Things were starting to fall into place.

Chapter 18

Nigel swayed slightly. "Think I need to sit for a minute," he announced, promptly plopping cross-legged onto the grass. "The world's gone a bit... spinny."

Einstein padded over, peering at him with the intensity of a scientific researcher. "The combined magical effects are fascinating," he said. "You should document this in the library for future reference."

"Not helpful," I muttered, crouching beside Nigel as he flopped onto his back, eyes fixed on the night sky.

"The sky is breathing," he informed me seriously. "Like it's alive."

Tom returned, his hands full of drinks. "That took longer than I expec..." His voice trailed off when he saw Nigel. "What's wrong with him?"

"Umm... he's had too much to drink," I lied.

Einstein let out a rumbling chuckle. "Or too much to eat!"

Tom shook his head and placed the cups on a nearby chair. "Come on, rookie," he said. "Let's get you home."

I nodded, scanning the square for a taxi to transport my magically overcooked witness. I did feel bad for Nigel, but he'd delivered some very interesting information.

Tom handed me the latte which should have been Nigel's.

"Who's your next lucky victim?" he asked. "Let's aim for someone who's still standing, and who doesn't want to tell us their life story in two minutes flat."

I gave a rueful smile. "No promises."

Tom laughed, but I was already scanning the crowd. "I've not spoken to Marcus or Vanessa," I told him. "And Nigel thought Daryl was bribing Marcus so the Stags would win. I'd like to know what they think about that."

"Hey! You can't blurt out a thing like that?" Tom said, his eyebrows shooting up in alarm.

I rolled my eyes. "Obviously. I'll be subtle."

"I can't see how you can be subtle about 'do you take bribes?'"

"The Langleys are staying at The Briar and Thorn," I said, ignoring him. "If I could find them..."

But by the time I'd finished my coffee, there was still no sign of either the judge or his wife on the village green.

"How about we try the pub's beer garden?" Tom suggested.

We set off, Murphy trotting ahead with purpose, while Einstein stalked beside me, tail high like he was personally overseeing the operation.

Fairy lights were strung overhead in loose arcs, glowing softly against the dark sky and giving the beer garden a gentle, golden haze. The scent of crushed grass and Scrumpy cider hung in the air, mingling with laughter, chatter and the faintest hint of fried onions.

Every bench and table was occupied. Clusters of competitors giggling over drinks, spectators recounting their favourite performances, the buzz of a day well spent still settling over the space.

From inside the pub, the Bodmin Barn Owls were belting out a lively rendition of *What Shall we do with the Drunken Sailor,* only they'd changed the lyrics to *Drunken Dancer,* and several members of the Dancing Hares were stomping out a chaotic, inebriated version of their competition routine in the doorway.

And then I spotted him.

Marcus Langley sat alone at the edge of the garden, one hand curled around a half-finished pint of ale, the other draped across the back of his bench. His posture was composed, but his eyes were distant.

He wasn't watching the dancing. He wasn't watching anything.

I nudged Tom. "Got him."

Tom followed my gaze. "You do know he's a lawyer."

"Lawyers are good at talking," I said, trying to sound breezy as I gathered my courage and my container of treats.

Tom raised an eyebrow. "Only when you're paying them."

I shrugged. "Then I won't be very long."

He nodded. "I'll hang around by the picnic tables. That way, I'll have your back, but far enough away not to crowd him."

"Thanks," I said.

As I made towards Marcus's table, Einstein fell into step beside me.

"You'll have to be careful with this one," my furry advisor cautioned. "Lawyers are trained to make you think they're being charming, but all the time they're saying nothing."

"Sounds like my lying, charming, nearly-ex-husband Gary," I groaned.

Up close, Marcus Langley was somehow more polished than he'd appeared from a distance. Every silver hair lay groomed, his shirt as crisp as if even the summer heat didn't dare to ruffle him.

I slid onto the bench opposite with what I hoped was a friendly smile. "Mind if I join you for a moment, Mr Langley? You look like someone in need of some home baking."

He gave me the kind of long-suffering expression usually reserved for witness boxes and tax returns.

"The shortbread's very good," I added cheerfully.

His gaze flicked past me toward the pub. The dancers were still merrily blocking the entrance. I could almost hear the silent debate playing out in his head: endure small talk with a chatty stranger or brave the gauntlet of the flailing elbows of Morris dancers mid-jig. For now, I appeared to be the lesser of the two evils.

I cracked open my tin of goodies and waved it under his nose. The warm, buttery scent did the rest. His shoulders eased, and the edge melted from his expression.

"Thank you."

He reached out long, manicured fingers, and there was the slightest hint of a pause before he selected a piece of shortbread. The caution of a man who didn't trust anything without a signed contract.

"Mmm." He took a bite, looking genuinely surprised it was edible.

I babbled about getting the ratio of butter to flour in the shortbread correct while I waited for the magic to encourage his mind to make connections and remember details. Marcus nodded, with the same level of interest you might offer to hedge-trimming.

By the time he'd finished most of the shortbread, Marcus's eyes had taken on the familiar, magical, glazed look.

I seized the opportunity to steer the conversation back to the afternoon's events.

"This is the first Morris dancing competition I've ever been to," I said enthusiastically.

As if sensing I was circling something more specific, Marcus's expression tightened.

"Don't push him," Einstein warned. "Remember, he's well trained in interrogation."

But I'd already gone too far.

Marcus sighed. "If you're about to ask about judging criteria, you'll be disappointed. I've had enough dancers sidle over for 'tips' to last me a lifetime. If I'd known adjudicating folk festivals involved this amount of begging and pleading, I'd have stuck to criminal arbitration."

I raised both hands in mock surrender. "No performance notes, I swear. I was only wondering what you made of the arrest. Do you think Eva's the murderer?"

Einstein's ears went flat. "What did I tell you about pushing things?" he muttered darkly beside my foot.

I crossed my fingers tightly under the table, hoping I hadn't blown it.

But Marcus brushed the crumbs from his shirt with meticulous care and sighed again. "I've watched enough cases unravel in court to know how deceptive appearances can be. Trust is a fragile thing," he said, his tone carrying the weight of someone who'd seen it all.

A flicker of recognition tightened in my stomach. Gary had been proof enough of that.

"But Eva always seems so straight down the line," I said carefully. "Everything I've seen her manage has been faultless."

"Oh, she's particular, all right," he agreed. "I've seen Eva across more village greens I care to count. Events she organises always run like clockwork." He swallowed the last of the shortbread. "Which is why I never thought I'd see the day when she handed the judges envelopes that didn't match, and that weren't even straight."

My pulse jumped.

"Of course, Ronald spotted the discrepancy in those ridiculous envelopes immediately," Marcus carried on. "Couldn't wait to point it out to Eva. He was a fair judge, but he liked to stir things up, you know? Had a real knack for it."

He gave a laugh that had no humour behind it.

"I tried to line the envelopes up myself. I wasn't in the mood for theatrics. But Ronald had already launched into one of his lectures. Him and Eva could never get along."

The gears in my brain clicked into place. Nigel had said Marcus was 'messing with the envelopes', but he hadn't been up to no good. He'd been straightening them to avoid a scene.

Did I believe that?

Yes, I think I did.

Of course, there was the vision of Vanessa I'd seen. But maybe it had nothing to do with the murder at all. Maybe it really had been Marcus looking at his wife.

Marcus reached for his ale. "They're saying it was the envelope that killed Ronald," he said. "Imagine if the wind hadn't blown them off the table? Imagine if they'd stayed in the order we started with?"

He took a long sip, then met my eyes and, for the first time, he looked tired.

"It would be me lying in that morgue."

I didn't say anything. I couldn't.

Because in that moment, the entire story twisted.

We'd all assumed Ronald had been the target. The loudest voice, the biggest ego, the man with the most enemies.

But what if he wasn't?

What if the poison had been meant for Marcus Langley?

Chapter 19

I STUDIED MARCUS CAREFULLY: the calm exterior, the precise mannerisms, the way he took another small sip of beer like he was trying to wash down his unease.

But I still had the issue of Daryl and the bribe. There was no easy way to say this.

"Did anyone ever try to... influence your scoring?" I asked as lightly as possible. "I've heard whispers. It's a close-knit village. People talk."

Marcus's mouth twitched. "They do indeed. And no one gossips better than a Morris dancer nursing a bruised ego after two pints."

I waited.

He glanced at me, then shook his head. "If you're fishing for something specific, Miss..."

"Appleton," I said. "Josie."

"Well, Miss Appleton, if you're suggesting someone tried to bribe me over bells and stick-work, you're barking up the wrong maypole." His voice sharpened. "This isn't a legal battle. I don't care who wins. I care that they dance in time and don't maim each other."

His shift in tone caught me off guard.

"I don't accept money or free drinks," he added, fixing me with a hard stare which I imagined won him closing arguments and unnerved entire courtrooms. "And you definitely don't get information by feeding me unsolicited muffins."

Yikes! He thought *I* was bribing him.

I gulped. "I'm sorry, Mr Langley, that was not my intention."

But I'd blown it. Marcus had had enough.

He stood up.

"Thank you for the shortbread, Miss Appleton," he said curtly, without even looking at me.

He made his way toward the pub entrance, which was now mercifully clear of rowdy dancers, the last piece of Nigel's bribery theory crumbling quietly in the corner of my brain.

Because, really, why would a wealthy lawyer accept money to throw a dancing competition? How much would Daryl have to pay him to make it worth his while?

Tom appeared at the table beside me. "Did you get any clues?" he asked.

"Well, I don't think Marcus is our murderer," I said. "He wasn't doing secret envelope swapping, and... I think that possibly the wrong person is dead."

"What?" Tom choked.

I told him what Marcus had said: every careful word.

"Trouble is," I added, "we know plenty of people who wanted Ronald gone. But who would want to kill Marcus Langley?"

We stared at each other over the table.

Neither of us had an answer.

The fairy lights cast gentle halos over empty glasses and half-eaten crisps, while from inside the pub the Bodmin Barn Owls tore through a fiddle tune so wild it sent two very drunk Merry Maids into a spinning frenzy which culminated in their dramatic tumble over the side fence.

Murphy let out a startled yelp at the commotion and bolted under the table, ears flattened, tail between his legs.

Einstein flicked his ears with disdain. "That," he muttered, "is why alcohol and complicated footwork should never mix."

"I think it's time we went back to the green," Tom said. "It's getting a bit chaotic in here."

I nodded, standing up. "That could've gone worse with Marcus," I said.

"You think?" Tom muttered. "I got a real 'courtroom closing remarks' vibe at the end."

Before I could reply, a familiar voice floated over the music.

"Evening, you two!" June Mercer, still in her Green Stags sash, waved a glass of wine our way. "You haven't seen Daryl, have you?"

"Not recently," I said, slowing to a stop. "Why?"

Geoff joined her. "We thought he'd be celebrating. He was so pumped after our win, but we haven't seen him for ages now."

June raised her eyebrows. "I figured he'd be with his girl-friend," she said. "Daryl's been rather mysterious lately. Always looking at his phone."

Geoff frowned. "I didn't know Daryl had a girlfriend. Well, not a serious one, anyway. I mean, he's always flirted with the girls. That's Daryl."

June gave a long-suffering sigh. "Oh, you never notice any-thing, do you, dear? How did you miss him texting non-stop on the minibus to Briarvale?" She looked at me. "I saw hearts, you know?"

Einstein gave a throaty chuckle. "Right, because nothing screams true love more than an electronic message with a heart emoji."

I tried to hide my smile.

"If I see him, I'll tell him you're looking for him," I assured June, and with that we made our escape.

Back out on the village green, people milled around the burg-er van and hog roast tent, plastic cups in hand, laughing and joking as though this afternoon's murder hadn't happened at all. The air was thick with the scent of charring meat, softened by the cool, faintly damp tang of the grass catching the night-time dew.

I glanced over at the makeshift stage. The judges' table was still ringed in police tape, a glitch in an otherwise perfect tableau. The stout officer I'd seen earlier still sat in the middle, his foot still propped on a chair while the young policewoman paced the perimeter with enough effort to make it look like she was working, although her attention was mostly on a group of the Black Boars attempting to build a kebab out of meat, chips and questionable drunken logic.

But there were two other figures at the stage. One was waving at us.

"Josie! Tom!"

Sally Barnes, cheeks flushed and hair wind-rustled, stood beside another officer in uniform, PC Jamie Waverley. Murphy perked up immediately, tail wagging, and he bounded over to say hello.

"Murphy remembers Jamie from the murder scene in your greenhouse," Tom said, as we crossed the grass toward them.

"Jamie wasn't even supposed to be on duty tonight," Sally explained before I could ask. "We were coming to watch the Bodmin Barn Owls. Mum's minding the kids. But then Jamie got the call from work." She gave me a lopsided smile. "At least we made it to the festival."

Jamie ruffled Murphy's fur. "Back-up for a Morris dance murder. Not how I pictured my evening, but here we are."

"All part of the job, I suppose," said Tom sympathetically.

"Oh!" said Jamie, eyeing the container I was carrying. "Is that what I think it is? Have you brought baking?"

"She has," Tom confirmed.

Jamie brightened. "Oh, I remember how good it was," he said enthusiastically. "Hey, Larry, Tasha, you've got to try this."

Einstein wound himself purposefully round my legs. "Toffee," he prompted me. "Give them the Loose-Tongue toffee. Find out what they know."

I nodded as I unhooked the lid. Only four pieces of toffee remained.

"The toffee needs finishing," I urged them. "It got rather warm in this box today."

"We can absolutely help you with that, ma'am," Jamie replied, selecting two pieces. He passed the largest one to Sally.

Einstein settled beside me. "You realise this is the equivalent of drugging the local constabulary," he commented.

The portly officer heaved himself off the chair. "Did someone say toffee?" he asked, plucking a piece from the tin. "Better than the ketchup-flavoured crisps Tasha was eating earlier."

"Hey. What was wrong with my crisps?" asked the young officer. She turned away from the Boars and their kebab sculptures and came over.

Larry accepted the offer of toffee with the enthusiasm of a child on Christmas morning. His eyes widened immediately he tasted it, a look of pure delight spreading across his face. "Good heavens," he exclaimed around the toffee, "this is extraordinary!"

"It *is* tasty," agreed Tasha. "Might even beat the ketchup crisps."

"This is Tasha's first time working a crime scene," Jamie told us.

"That's exciting," I said. "How are you enjoying it?"

"Great," Tasha said, her Cornish lilt rising and falling like waves. "Didn't think I'd be on a murder case so soon, but it's been brilliant being part of it all."

"Too right," Larry added with a laugh that came from deep in his chest. "I get to sit here at the festival and get paid for it." He swallowed the last of his toffee. "The only thing better than that is fishing."

"Larry does talk about fishing rather a lot," Tasha admitted, with a guilty look in Larry's direction.

"Here we go," chortled Einstein. "Confession time."

"Seven types of bait," Tasha continued, the words tumbling out. "He went on about seven types of bait for thirty minutes straight. I timed it."

"Cheeky little whipper-snapper," said Larry, with a good-natured laugh.

His police radio crackled to life, spitting static and a garbled voice that miraculously he somehow translated into language. He excused himself with a brief nod and stepped away, still savouring the last remnants of toffee.

"Well," said Jamie, "DI Holloway told us the lab confirmed cyanide poisoning. It was on the envelope Burrows licked," he added enthusiastically, the toffee's magic loosening his usually professional discretion.

Then, as if suddenly remembering himself, he straightened his posture, though the effect was undermined by the lump of toffee bulging in his cheek. "But that's confidential information, so don't go telling anyone. I shouldn't really have told you."

Einstein rolled his eyes. "And yet, you did."

Sally turned toward Jamie. "Cyanide? That's... proper serious," she said. Then, without missing a beat, she added brightly, "Also, I really like you."

She clapped a hand over her mouth.

"You do?" Jamie turned pink from the collar of his uniform right up to his ears. For a heartbeat, he stared at her, his eyes wide, his expression caught somewhere between delight and disbelief. Then, with a stunned sort of decisiveness, he leaned in and kissed her.

It wasn't long, but it was definitely not nothing.

Sally made a soft, startled sound, and then kissed him back.

Tom and I looked at each other. This was getting awkward.

Einstein chuckled again. "Your magic's working a treat," he said. "He'll be down on one knee next. Possibly still chewing toffee."

Larry returned, his ruddy face a shade redder than usual. He took a look at Sally and Jamie, still tangled in the aftermath of their kiss, and cleared his throat.

"Alright, you two. Umm, best save that for off-duty hours," he said, eyeing them with mock sternness. "DI Holloway's on his way. There's been a development in the case."

Chapter 20

"IT'S ODD THE DI's coming back, isn't it?" I asked, trying to sound merely curious rather than investigatively nosy.

Larry shrugged, his shoulders rising and falling beneath his rather too-tight uniform. "Something about Mrs Henshaw kicking up a fuss about the envelope. Not that I should be telling you this," he admitted, running his fingers through his thinning hair. "Don't know what's wrong with me tonight. Can't keep my mouth shut."

"Especially about fishing," Tasha cut in, then immediately clamped her hand over her mouth, eyes wide with horror at what she'd said.

Luckily, Larry simply chuckled. "That's what my wife says," he said cheerfully.

I watched them amble back towards the judges' table, still chatting about the best time of day to catch mackerel and whether the DI had ever smiled in his life.

Sally, who had been unashamedly holding Jamie's hand, gave it a squeeze. "I suppose I should go, if your DI's on his way."

"Don't go far," Jamie said with a wink.

Tom and I turned away as Jamie leaned in for another kiss, in time to watch one of the Springleaf Ramblers attempt a spin and promptly scatter their chips like confetti.

We both laughed.

Percy and Edwin were walking across the green too. That was when Charlie spotted Einstein.

Or possibly smelled him. Hard to say which came first, but the result was immediate. With the delighted shriek of a creature who has rediscovered his sworn enemy, the little Shorkie launched into motion, bouncing on the end of his lead in an unnecessary battle with gravity and restraint.

Einstein watched him disdainfully. "That dog is so embarrassing," he groaned.

Charlie, predictably, lost his mind. The teddy-bear-with-battery-pack let out a squealing war cry and lunged, dragging Percy behind him like a man caught water-skiing behind an out-of-control motorboat.

Einstein, calmly assessing the incoming threat, turned on his paw and trotted casually in the opposite direction.

"Charlie! No!" Percy yelled.

When Charlie didn't slow, Einstein picked up speed, his tail held high. In one graceful movement he leapt onto the stage between Larry and Tasha and vanished behind the table.

Charlie responded with a yank so sudden that Percy staggered sideways, and with one last yelp of triumph from the dog, the lead slipped from his fingers.

"Come here!" Percy cried, uselessly.

But Charlie was unstoppable, his little legs a blur of fluff and vengeance.

Fortunately, Jamie took on the attack with the speed of a seasoned midfielder. He darted forward, sidestepping Sally and an abandoned cider cup. Charlie zigged to the right. Jamie blocked him. Charlie zagged to the left, and Jamie executed a clean, sweeping scoop, catching Charlie mid-air as he launched onto the plywood ramp. He cradled Charlie, a pint-sized runaway football in his arms.

"Got him!" called Jamie, as Percy huffed up to the stage.

Charlie barked indignantly, his legs still paddling the air in protest.

Einstein, now perched loftily on the judges' table gave a delicate sniff, radiating the unmistakable air of a stadium commentator unimpressed with the team's performance.

"Decent form from the police officer," he noted. "But honestly, I was starting to root for the dog."

Jamie returned the squirming bundle to Percy, who was busy straightening his shirt.

"Sorry about that," he puffed. "Charlie has a thing about cats."

Einstein leaped lightly from the stage.

"The feeling is mutual," he purred sweetly.

I watched little Charlie's pink tongue loll, his ears perked, his enthusiasm undimmed.

And something clicked.

"Charlie ran off like this earlier," I said aloud. "Right before the contest."

Tom tilted his head. "He is a tricky little cutie."

"Yes, but Daryl caught him," I said, my stomach tightening. "He was standing there on the stage. After Eva had put all the envelopes and score cards out for the judges."

Tom's eyes met mine.

And just like that, another piece of the mystery dropped into place.

"I have to speak to Daryl," I said, taking off across the grass towards The Briar and Thorn at speed.

Tom hurried to catch me.

"I thought you didn't believe Nigel about Daryl bribing the judges."

"He wasn't bribing them," I said. "He was murdering them."

"What?" Tom spluttered. "Why?"

"If we assume that the poison was meant for Marcus, Vanessa might have paid Daryl to do it," I suggested, not slowing down.

The Bodmin Barn Owls were well into their final set and the sound of fiddles and guitars and drums grew louder as we neared the pub.

Hoping that I wouldn't have to fight my way into the bar to find Daryl or Vanessa, I veered towards the beer garden first. I pushed open the side gate, only to almost collide with Pippa.

"Ooh, sorry," I gasped.

Pippa had a tray balanced on one arm, stacked high with glasses. She steadied it with a practiced flick of her wrist.

"No harm done," she said, giving a weary sigh. "But I'll be glad when tonight's over, though. My legs hate me, and my feet are filing for separation."

"Poor you," I said with a sympathetic smile. "But hey!" I went on as she turned to return to her glass collection duties. "You never finished telling me about the Langleys earlier."

Pippa paused, leaning her hip against the table. "Oh, those two. Yeah. Right." She lowered her voice. "Let's put it this way, they're not exactly the romantic getaway types. Honestly, I've seen more warmth from a fridge."

I hid a grin, but Tom chuckled under his breath.

Pippa glanced over her shoulder, then leaned closer. "They barely speak to each other unless someone's around," she went on. "Polite, polished... but cold. Makes you wonder what goes on behind closed doors."

She absently arranged the glasses on the tray in size order.

"And this morning," she added, "I was out by the bins with some empties. Glamorous, I know. But who do I spot loitering near the back entrance?" She arched an eyebrow. "Vanessa. And that handsome guy from the Green Stags."

"Daryl," Tom and I said together.

Pippa tapped her temple. "They thought there were being subtle. Vanessa was doing the 'touch his arm and laugh' thing." She lowered her voice. "And Daryl? Preening like a peacock. The man was practically smouldering at her. If flirtation were a contact sport, they'd have needed a time-out and a referee."

"Whoa," said Tom. "This is getting spicy."

Einstein huffed beneath the table. "Pompous posturing and purring nonsense. Feral cats have more self-respect."

Pippa grinned. "And you'll love this bit," she said. "Before they saw me, Vanessa passed him an envelope. Totally casual, like she was handing him his wallet or something." She mimed the handover with a flick. "But the way he tucked it under his jacket, it might've been the winning lottery ticket." She widened her eyes. "Or a lover's gift."

Tom and I exchanged glances.

"Told you," Pippa grinned. "This is my pub. I see every-thing."

"Don't suppose you know where Daryl and Vanessa are now?" I asked.

"Well, I haven't seen Vanessa much at all tonight, but earlier, Daryl was mooching around the door to the upstairs rooms for a while. I think he was looking for her," Pippa told me, with a knowing wink. "But he was sitting by the door with the other Green Stags nursing a pint when I came out for the glasses. Honestly, he doesn't look all that thrilled for someone who's won the Morris dancing for the second year in a row."

Pippa continued with her glass collection, and I looked at Tom.

He didn't say a word. He didn't need to.

If Vanesa was the secret girlfriend that June suspected Daryl had, then this crime wasn't about dancing competitions, or even revenge. It was about love. And that made this murder a whole lot more dangerous.

Chapter 21

I TURNED TOWARDS THE pub, my pulse quickening.

There was only one muffin and one piece of short-bread left, so I had to be very careful, but it was time to hear Daryl's side of the story.

However, as I reached for the door handle, Tom caught my arm.

"If Daryl poisoned the envelope, this could be risky," he said, his eyes concerned. "Don't you think that you should wait for DI Holloway and tell him what you know?"

"Well..." I started.

It made sense, but then I'd really like to present an airtight case to the inspector, especially after his steely warning to keep my nose out.

Einstein pushed against my leg. "And the floor's too sticky for a cat's furry feet."

I frowned at him. "No. I still think I should speak to Daryl," I said. "To make sure. I wouldn't want to look stupid in the eyes of DI Leave-This-to-the-Professionals Holloway."

"Oh, my goodness," Tom sighed. "You are as headstrong as your grandmother. Once she got an idea in her head, there was no shifting her." He gestured vaguely toward the pub. "She once staged a sit-in at the WI AGM because they tried to ban homemade lemon curd. Brought a flask, a footstool, and didn't budge for six hours."

Einstein wound round my legs. "I remember that day," he said. "They surrendered after I started sharpening my claws on the vicar's chair."

I laughed. "But I'm still going to talk to Daryl."

The pub was comfortably warm, alive with laughter and the hum of conversation. The Bodmin Barn Owls were closing out their set, their music mellowed into something swayable. Couples slow-danced wherever they found room: by the fireplace, between tables, near the fruit machine.

As Pippa had said, the members of the Green Stags were tucked into the corner near the door. Their winners' cup gleamed in the middle of the table surrounded by a collection of mostly-empty glasses.

Einstein placed a furry paw delicately over the threshold.

"Excellent," he said. "There's minimal distance to the Green Stags. Limited floor contact necessary."

Murphy gave a cheerful bark and wiggled through the crowd to the table without bumping a soul. I followed in his wake, Tom at my shoulder.

"Josie! Tom!" June's eyes lit up as soon as she spotted us.

Geoff leaned back in his chair, smiling as Murphy licked his hand. "You brought the dog!" he beamed.

"And the cat," June added, as Einstein leapt gracefully onto the bench beside her. "I've never seen a cat in a pub before."

"That's because most cats have standards," sighed Einstein. "Mine have to be negotiable when murder is involved."

I glanced around. "Did you ever find Daryl? Last time we spoke you were looking for him."

"Oh yes," Geoff said. "He turned up not long after we saw you."

June made a face. "But he was in a mood. Sat right there." She gestured to the empty chair on the opposite side of the table. "Miserable as sin, he was. I reckon he'd had a lover's tiff."

Geoff shook his head. "You and your theories."

"Did he say where he was going?" I asked.

Geoff shrugged. "The bar? The loo?"

Tom scanned the room: the bar, the alcoves, and every occupied chair.

"No sign of him," he murmured. "I'll check the toilets."

While he slipped away, Einstein picked his way delicately around the cluttered table. He reached the now-vacant seat where June had told us Daryl had been sitting and settled on the cushion. He sniffed at the table, then at the chair, his nose low, his tail a furry antenna.

He paused. Sniffed again. Then stood up, back arched.

"That's it!" he announced triumphantly, his tail swishing with excitement. "I knew I recognised the other scent on the envelopes' box. As well as cyanide, there was Daryl's aftershave. He reeked of it when he came into Briarwood Gables this morning. My nose was tingling for hours afterwards."

My stomach clenched. The last piece fell into place. If Daryl had handled the poisoned envelope, it made perfect sense that his strong-smelling aftershave would have transferred to the paper.

June yawned. "I think we're beginning to feel our age," she said, stretching. "Once we've finished our drinks, it's back to Briarwood Gables. It's been a lovely day, but it's catching up with me now."

"You've got your key, right?" I said, suddenly worried I'd have to leave the investigation before I'd handed everything over to DI Holloway.

Geoff patted his pocket. "On my keyring,"

I sighed with relief. "Hope you sleep well, and I'll see you at breakfast tomorrow."

June smiled. "Don't expect us down too early."

Tom returned and shook his head.

No Daryl.

We made our way outside as the final note from the Bodmin Barn Owls was swallowed by the rapturous applause from the audience.

I was sure I knew who the murderer was. But to prove it I needed to find Daryl and Vanessa.

If I couldn't, I'd have to settle for giving my clues to the DI.

Somehow, the truth had to come out. I wasn't about to let the police prosecute Eva for a crime she didn't commit.

Chapter 22

THE EVENING AIR WAS cooler now, and I was glad I'd brought my jacket. People were spilling out of The Briar and Thorn, making a bee-line for the snack vans in search of post-pub sustenance. Unfortunately, they didn't include either Vanessa or Daryl.

"We should go back to the crime scene," I said to Tom. "To wait for the DI."

We'd just passed the hog roast tent when a slender figure stomped into view from behind the burger stall. Cream blouse, tailored trousers and a walk that said the day had pushed its luck one time too many.

Vanessa Langley.

She paused nearby, her movements stiff with tension, her hands fumbling with a silver cigarette case.

A moment later, a man emerged behind her.

Daryl.

He approached with the confident swagger of a man used to sweet-talking his way out of trouble, but when he reached for her arm, she jerked away.

Her voice was low and sharp, and although I didn't hear the words, I caught their meaning. Daryl's shoulders slumped like someone had punched the air out of him. He turned and headed off toward the pub.

"Did you see that?" I asked, tugging Tom's sleeve.

"What?"

I kept my eyes on Vanessa. "Never mind. Oh wait! No. Actually, can you follow Daryl? We don't want to lose him again."

Tom raised an eyebrow, but he nodded. "I'll check out where he's going." With Murphy trotting dutifully at his side, he disappeared into the crowd.

I turned towards Vanessa.

Beside me, Einstein's ears went flat. "Really?" he grumbled. "We're approaching the angry woman with the fire-and-poison sticks?"

"Shush," I muttered, smoothing my expression into what I hoped was a sympathetic smile.

"Trouble with the lighter?" I asked, stepping closer and retrieving a Truth-Whispering Muffin from my container. "Would a snack help? I still have some left."

Vanessa's gaze flicked from my face to the muffin, suspicion warring with hunger in her eyes. But after a moment, she snatched it and took an angry bite.

"Is *that* with you?" she asked, pointing toward Einstein with a manicured finger.

"That!?" Einstein bristled. "The correct pronoun is 'who,' you pretentious..."

"Yes. He's with me," I cut in quickly, giving him a gentle nudge with my foot. "His name's Einstein."

"Ridiculous name for a cat," Vanessa said, exhaling a stream of smoke in the opposite direction.

"He happens to be a rather clever cat," I replied, as she took another bite of the muffin.

I needed to keep her talking until the magic took hold.

"I'm sure he is," she said with a bored sigh.

"Rough night?" I ventured.

"You could say that," she replied, through a mouthful of muffin. The truth spell was working. She was beginning to loosen her tight grip on control.

"I can relate," I said, testing the waters. "My husband abandoned me with nothing but the clothes on my back."

"That's pitiful," she said.

Her words landed like a slap.

That was harsh.

"I hate useless, weak women," she added, looking me up and down with undisguised distaste, as if my very existence offended her.

If I hadn't wanted the intel, I would have left her to stew by herself. But I couldn't resist muttering, "Don't hold anything back on my account," under my breath.

"You have to stand up for yourself," she went on, the muffin's magic encouraging her natural tendency toward brutal honesty, or was that plain rudeness. "Make sure you're compensated if someone wrongs you. Marcus was planning to cut me out of his will! Can you believe that?"

Her eyes widened, the barest shift, but I saw it. She'd said more than she'd meant to.

The magic had her.

But I was inwardly reeling at the bitterness pouring out from such a polished exterior.

"No," Vanessa continued, taking another aggressive bite of my baking. "You must take matters into your own hands, so to speak." She paused, a small, secretive smile playing at the corners of her mouth. "Use them, before they use you."

"I'll remember that," I said lightly. "Oh, sorry, I haven't introduced myself properly," I hurried on. "I'm Josie."

"Vanessa," she said, with a slight smirk that suggested she knew perfectly well that everyone would know who she was.

"Yes, I know," I replied, deciding honesty might encourage more of the same from her. "I saw you earlier with Marcus."

Vanessa laughed, a sound as sharp and cold as breaking icicles. "Ah, my inattentive, scheming husband, you mean?"

My surprise at her scathing remark must have been obvious, because her smile broadened with satisfaction.

"Oh, you think that's shocking?" she asked.

The fairy lights caught the highlights in her expensively maintained hair, turning them momentarily to fire as she tossed her head.

"I was supposed to be leaving for our villa in Italy next week. Enrico's a very handsome man. Very passionate. Very *not* my husband." Her expression softened for a moment, then it hardened again. "But everything got messed up. So, I'm still stuck with the world's most romantically uninteresting man this side of Watford Gap Service Station."

I did a double take. She was leaving with some guy called Enrico?

Were all those love hearts June had seen Daryl sending not meant for Vanessa at all?

Had Vanessa simply paid Daryl to poison Marcus?

But in my vision, Daryl had looked at Vanessa with genuine feelings. It was more likely she was stringing him along, using him as a fall guy for Marcus's murder. Then she would disappear into the sunset with her Italian lover.

Vanessa popped the last of the muffin in her mouth, brushing crumbs from her blouse in precise, angry movements. "And I'm here in this sad excuse for a hotel..."

She dropped her cigarette and ground it out with the toe of her designer shoe, then began to walk toward the pub. After a few steps, she turned, looking back at me with a smile that didn't reach her eyes.

"...At least, for now," she finished.

Then she wiggled her fingers in a mock-cheerful wave.

"Time to get my beauty sleep and work on Plan B. Toodaloo," she said.

Vanessa walked towards the side door of The Briar and Thorn, but then she noticed Daryl loitering there and veered sharply, slipping through the front entrance instead.

What she didn't notice was Tom. He was talking to Sally and amiably throwing the ball for Murphy, while keeping his eye on Daryl.

I watched her go, feeling as though I'd had a close encounter with something beautiful but deadly.

Einstein's tail twitched. "Wow," he said. "That woman is one book short of a series."

I couldn't help but grin.

"Your sleuthing skills are really improving," he added, with a flick of his whiskers. "At this rate, you'll have them confessing to the police, like your grandmother did with that marrow champion murder she solved."

I shook my head, half-amused, half-shocked at his compliment, a plan already forming.

But before I got it straight, a car pulled onto the green, headlights sweeping across the grass to the cordon on the stage.

DI Holloway had arrived.

Chapter 23

I HURRIED TOWARDS THE stage, heading off Detective Inspector Holloway before he reached it.

The DI stopped dead when he saw me. His eyebrows drew together in a frown that emphasised the stern lines of his face, and for a moment his professional mask cracked enough to reveal genuine irritation.

"Ms Appleton?" he said, not even trying to hide the disapproval in his voice.

"Detective Inspector," I greeted him cheerfully, pretending I hadn't noticed his annoyance.

Behind him, on the stage, Jamie Waverley nudged Larry, who turned round eating a doughnut.

"I assume," Holloway said, with a sigh that sounded like it came from deep inside his soul, "that given your presence here, you did *not* follow my advice about staying out of the investigation."

I smiled sweetly, enjoying the slight twitch of annoyance at the corner of his eye.

"Umm, not really," I said. "Sorry."

Einstein padded round the detective and sat down so he was facing me. "Try to sound a little bit apologetic," he advised. "And not simply smug."

I tried, but a smile slipped through.

"But I know who the killer is," I said boldly, deciding to seize the opportunity rather than dance around it. "Or, should I say, killers."

DI Holloway folded his arms across his chest, his lean frame silhouetted against the festival lights, his posture radiating suspicion and exasperation in equal measures.

"Really," he said, the word emerging as a sigh, not a proper acknowledgment. "I suppose you're going to tell me anyway, so let's get it over with."

I drew a breath, my heart beating faster. "It was Daryl King, the leader of the Green Stags Morris dance troupe, and Vanessa Langley," I told him. "They were both in the plan together."

DI Holloway's expression didn't change, but I saw a flicker of interest beneath the scepticism.

"Vanessa bought the envelope from Fletcher's store. I'm not sure who added the cyanide to it, but Daryl was on the stage before the contest began," I blurted. "I think that's when he swapped the poisoned envelope into Marcus's spot."

"Wait! Marcus Langley?" interrupted the DI. "Miss Appleton, the victim was Ronald Burrows."

"Yes, but it wasn't supposed to be Ronald," I explained patiently. "The wind blew the envelopes off the table, and when Eva picked them up, the fatal envelope ended up in front of Ronald by mistake."

Behind us, Jamie now had his arms crossed, watching. Larry had forgotten about finishing his doughnut, and Tasha wasn't even pretending not to listen.

Holloway's brow furrowed. "So, why target Mr Langley?" he asked.

"Vanessa was planning to leave her husband and run off with some Italian guy named Enrico," I explained. "But Marcus is a lawyer. She knew she would never get a decent divorce settlement. So, she cooked up a getaway plan to kill him and take everything."

"And Daryl King?" said Holloway. His voice was still sceptical, but the sharp edge had gone. "What does he get out of this arrangement?"

"Well, Pippa from The Briar and Thorn saw Vanessa passing Daryl something this morning," I told him. "That was probably when she gave him the poisoned envelope. But it could have been money. Or a love note. Maybe both. I think Vanessa was flirting with Daryl so he'd do the dirty work, leaving her in the clear."

"You've been a busy bee, Ms Appleton," said the DI. "What part of 'don't get involved' wasn't clear to you?"

"You arrested Eva," I said, folding my arms to match him. "I couldn't let you charge the wrong person."

"Firstly," the DI bristled, "Eva was not under arrest. She was merely being questioned."

"And did those questions lead you to Daryl and Vanessa?"

He drew a breath, then stilled.

Einstein jumped up in uncharacteristic excitement.

"You've got him," he mewed.

Tasha gave a small jump, Jamie blinked, and Larry dropped what was left of his doughnut.

I looked back at Holloway and smiled. "So, are you ready to catch them? Because I have a plan to get them to confess."

Einstein's eyes widened in surprise.

"Hey! Are you thinking of your grandmother's marrow champion murder?" he commented, with the smugness of a cat who knew full well he'd sharpened the clue into shape. "Because I gave you that idea."

I grinned.

"A plan?" Holloway repeated flatly, as though I'd proposed we communicate via interpretive dance.

His shoulders slumped, the gesture so out of character that I knew I'd won.

"Fine. What's your plan?" he said, in the weary tone that suggested he already regretted asking.

I leaned forward, excitement bubbling up. "You request to talk to Daryl and Vanessa. You get them out here together. I'll be nearby, but not obviously part of the questioning."

The DI's expression remained unconvinced, but he didn't interrupt.

"You ask them something like where were they this morning? And then you'll get a call...my call," I continued. "You step away, saying it's urgent. I sit down. They admit what they've done. But here's the clever part," I held up my phone, waggling it slightly, "you'll still be on the line. You'll be listening to everything they say to me. You can record the call as evidence, and when they confess..."

I caught his raised eyebrow at my confidence.

"...which they will," I added. "Then you can step back in and make the arrest."

The detective studied me with narrowed eyes, considering every word. "So basically, in this plan, I do... nothing," he said.

"No, you are crucial," I insisted. "You're the reason they'll sit down in the first place. You get the recording. You get the arrest. And of course, you get all the credit."

DI Holloway didn't speak for a long moment. His fingers drummed a silent rhythm against his thigh, while the festival buzzed around us.

"It's a good plan," I said. "And what's more, you have nothing to lose. If I'm right, you catch the killers, and if I'm wrong... I'll never get involved with another investigation, ev-er."

Einstein sat up straight at that. "Whoa!" he chimed in. "Risky promise."

All eyes were on the detective: mine, Jamie's, Larry's, Tasha's, even Einstein's.

The moment stretched between us, DI Holloway's calculating gaze weighing my proposal against his professional instincts.

The idea of having me out of his hair in the future was clearly appealing to him. He uncrossed his arms. Shifted his weight.

"Come on," I pressed. "It's a win-win situation."

"We'd have to locate Mr King and Mrs Langley..." the DI started.

"Vanessa went into The Briar and Thorn not ten minutes ago," I told him efficiently. "And Daryl's round at the side door. Tom's keeping an eye on him."

He rolled his eyes. "Of course he is."

He fixed me with a hard stare. "And if this plan of yours doesn't work," he said finally, his tone leaving no doubt which outcome he expected, "you will leave all future investigating to the police."

"You have my word."

The DI took a deep breath, the sound of a man preparing to step out onto thin ice.

"OK," he said with an air of resignation. "Go on. Let's give it your best shot."

His tone was flat, but I didn't care.

I'd won.

All I had to do was hope the last Truth-Whispering Muffins would work their magic.

Chapter 24

DETECTIVE INSPECTOR HOLLOWAY TURNED to Jamie and Larry. "PC Waverley, PC Higgins. Fetch Mr King and Mrs Langley over here, please?"

I moved away from the stage: far enough from the police cordon to look casual, close enough to observe what was going on.

While I waited, I bent down to talk to Einstein.

"There are only two muffins left," I whispered, patting the container. "Think it'll harm Vanessa if she has a second? I mean, it won't make her start rhyming like Liam did, will it? And I don't want a repeat of the Nigel the-sky-is-breathing fiasco. But it's going to look odd if I offer one to Liam but refuse to let her have another."

Einstein considered this. He was sitting in a perfect sphinx pose, his tail curled neatly around his body. "Liam overdosed on Loose-Tongue Toffee, and Nigel mixed the magic spells by eating one of everything," he said slowly. "Feeding Vanessa two of the same should, in theory, simply enhance the effects of the magic." He flicked his tail. "However, it will also make the woman more rude and intolerable. That'll be bad enough."

"True," I agreed.

"Remember," he advised, "don't force things. Keep it casual. Maybe reveal something that sets them against each other."

"Good idea," I nodded.

If I could get them to turn on each other, the muffin might do the rest.

Across the green, I spotted Larry with Daryl.

Daryl moved with his usual swagger, but there was a tension in his shoulders.

Relieved of their surveillance duties, Tom and Murphy followed them at a distance. Sally walked beside them, wide-eyed with interest at stumbling into the middle of a crime drama.

"What's going on?" Tom asked.

He and Sally sat on the grass next to me.

"I'm guessing you're involved?" he said.

"'Fraid so."

Tom shook his head in disbelief. "You are such a surprising woman, Josie Appleton," he said.

A hot flush crept up my neck.

Did he mean surprising in a good way? Or surprising in a she's-one-shortbread-away-from-a-crazy-woman way? The way my father used to think of my grandmother.

Sally was looking at me with a told-you-he-liked-you kind of grin.

But I didn't have time to unpack that thought, because Daryl and Larry had reached DI Holloway.

"I'm sorry to drag you away from the festivities, Mr King," the detective was saying to Daryl. "This won't take a moment. I'm just waiting for my colleague."

"Well, I hope it doesn't take too long," said Daryl stiffly. "Otherwise, the others will go back to the B&B in the minibus without me, and I'll have to walk."

I glanced at Sally and Tom.

"If this plays out how I think it will," I whispered, "then Daryl won't be going back to Briarwood Gables at all. He'll be heading for a jail cell."

"Way to lose one of your first paying customers," Tom grimaced. "At least it'll be one guest less to cater for breakfast."

I looked at him.

Amongst the murder and the investigation, I'd almost forgotten about real life.

Producing breakfast for my guests might be more stressful than catching a killer.

But the village drama wasn't done yet.

We didn't have long to wait before Jamie Waverley appeared out of the pub with Vanessa. She moved with elegance, her expression giving nothing away, but, judging by the arch of her brows and poor Jamie's harried expression, she was still in full speak-your-mind venom mode. The Truth-Whispering Muffins weren't changing her; they were simply removing any filters. Jamie looked as though he wished he'd brought back-up.

Einstein mewed loudly. "She's a wasp in lip gloss," he muttered. "Remind me to disinfect the muffin tin later."

When Daryl caught sight of her, his shoulders tensed even more. Vanessa, however, didn't break her stride. She stopped beside him, leaving a careful distance between them.

"What's this nonsense all about?" she snapped at DI Holloway. "I trust you understand my husband is a lawyer?"

The DI gave her a tight-lipped smile. "That I do, Mrs Langley," he said. "I have one or two questions I need to ask, that's all. It shouldn't take long."

Another flush crept up my neck. I was about to step onto a stage with no lines and a live audience.

"Please take a seat," DI Holloway continued, gesturing to the chairs by the judges' table.

Vanessa perched on the edge of one, as if concerned about contaminating her expensive clothing, while Daryl slouched beside her. The tension in his jaw spoiled his illusion of cool confidence.

Holloway sat down, too. "Could you both tell me where you were before the competition started?"

I'd half-expected him to abandon the plan at the last minute, but he was sticking to it to the letter.

I gripped my phone and pressed dial.

His mobile buzzed immediately, and he made a show of checking the screen, his acting far more convincing than I'd expected.

"Sorry," he said to Daryl and Vanessa, with realistic-looking reluctance. "I have to take this." He moved several paces away, far enough to be out of earshot but with a clear view of the proceedings.

Einstein stretched, and then in a flash of inspired sleuthing, he strolled across the grass. He paused near Vanessa's heels, gave Daryl a slow, withering once-over, and hopped onto the table. His tail swept from side to side like a metronome as he sat down and fixed them with an amber-eyed stare.

Sally raised an eyebrow. "It's almost like Einstein knew that's what you wanted him to do," she said. "Have you trained him?"

I grinned. "Depends who you ask," I said. "But it looks as though I'm going to have to retrieve him," I said, scrambling to my feet.

I crossed the grass, the last two muffins sliding gently around inside the tin, and my heart pounding.

"Come on, Einstein," I called, as if this wasn't all brilliantly choreographed. "Off the table, please."

He flicked an ear but remained where he was.

Of course not. The show was only beginning.

I reached the table, gently lifting him down, and gave Vanessa and Daryl a warm smile.

"Sorry about my cat," I said sweetly. "He likes to be part of the conversation."

Vanessa gave me a look that would curdle custard, but Daryl chuckled, leaning back.

"Aww, he's alright. Bit of an overweight, fluff ball, isn't he?"

Einstein turned his head and locked eyes with him. It was the kind of stare that suggested if he'd been an actual witch, instead of a familiar, Daryl would be spending the rest of his life as a damp toad on a lily pad.

"Overweight!" he yowled, scandalised. "And I am not fluffy. I am a particularly fine specimen of a pedigree Persian."

With a snort of offence and a majestic swish of his tail, he stalked off, every step announcing that the situation was beneath him.

I edged away too. Then, in a performance worthy of an Oscar, I turned back, as if I'd had a sudden flash of inspiration.

"I've got two muffins left," I told them. "Do you want to finish them?"

Daryl leaned forward immediately. "Now you're talking," he grinned.

Even Vanessa sat up straighter and nodded her head with enthusiasm.

My plan had seemed brilliant in theory. But faced with two potential killers and only a couple of magical muffins between us, I felt a flutter of doubt.

From the corner of my eye, I could see the DI watching, his phone pressed to his ear, waiting for me to deliver on my confident promises.

Einstein purred. Tom offered a subtle thumbs-up, while Sally gave me a wide-eyed grin and clasped her hands together, as if she was about to watch her favourite part of a very good play.

Their confidence boosted me.

I wasn't alone in this.

I took a deep breath.

It was time to begin the final act of this village drama.

Chapter 25

T HE LAST SCRAPS OF the festival crowd were drifting home now, paper cups in hand, gossip in the air,
while I stood beneath the fading bunting, extending the tin of
Truth-Whispering Muffins toward Vanessa and Daryl as though
it was a usual village courtesy.

Daryl immediately took a huge bite of his while Vanessa nib-
bled delicately at the edge of hers.

I could sense the strain between them. All I had to do was
earn their trust and give the muffin's magic a moment to take
effect.

"Between you and me," I said, leaning forward as if sharing a
secret, "I don't think the detective over there could catch a cold,
even if it had one leg and was hopping through treacle."

"He certainly has the charm of a traffic bollard," Vanessa
said crisply. "Although I expect a traffic bollard might ask better
questions."

Daryl let out a laugh, genuine and surprised. For a moment, their mutual disdain for the law was something they agreed on.

I glanced at the DI, who had turned rather red around the collar and was angrily signalling for me to get on with it. The man clearly wasn't accustomed to improvisation.

"Well done, Josie," came Einstein's voice from beneath the table, where he'd strategically positioned himself. "Now, easy does it."

"I can't believe somebody killed Mr Burrows," I said, casually.

Daryl and Vanessa exchanged a brief glance. It was gone in a heartbeat, but I caught it.

Did the muffins need more time?

Or perhaps another prod?

"The police think there was poison on the envelope. Can you believe that?" I added, widening my eyes for effect. "I mean, how would that even work?"

"Well, I'd put it on the bit you lick," Daryl replied, the words tumbling out before he was able to stop them.

He winced. Too late.

Vanessa turned and glared at him.

"Not that I did that, of course," Daryl added, rubbing a hand over his face.

"So close," mewed Einstein.

Time to stir the hornet's nest.

"So, Vanessa," I said, conversationally, "when did you say you were flying out to Italy with Enrico?"

Vanessa spun toward me with a look that would have frozen hell.

"Who the heck is Enrico?" Daryl demanded, the muffins making him incapable of holding back his reaction.

"Just a guy," Vanessa told him. Her mouth was set in a hard, unmoving line.

Daryl leaned in, his voice rising. "Oh! So, what am I, then?"

The sound of the festival faded into the background as the air round our table changed, and out of the corner of my eye I saw DI Holloway straighten up.

"*You* are the guy who messed everything up," Vanessa snapped, every word loaded to hurt. "You are the reason we're still in this ridiculous little village."

"Hey!" Daryl shoved back his chair, and I glimpsed Tom stand up on the grass.

"I am so sick of you blaming me for the stupid wind," Daryl shouted.

Vanessa hissed through her teeth, shooting a sideways glance at the DI, who was now slowly making his way back toward our table. His movements were deliberately unhurried, but purposeful.

"Shut. Up. Daryl," she said, low and furious. "You might as well tell them you put the envelope there yourself."

"Well, it was your stupid idea," Daryl shot back. "And I'll tell you what guy I am." He jabbed a finger at Vanessa. "I'm the guy who took all the risks for you. I'm the guy who had to sneak to the judges' table and swap the envelopes. You didn't even get the right sized envelope, so don't you dare..."

But then he stopped as DI Holloway arrived beside them, his arms folded.

"Well then," he said. "That was unexpectedly interesting."

He let the silence stretch for a beat longer than comfort allowed.

"And as for the comparison to a traffic bollard, Mrs Langley, I think you'll find that they're rather good at stopping people."

"You idiot!" snarled Vanessa, lashing out at Daryl's arm.

Daryl flinched, and all the colour drained out of his face.

Larry and Tasha stepped up behind Daryl and Vanessa, their earlier friendliness now replaced with professionalism.

DI Holloway cleared his throat. "Daryl King and Vanessa Langley, I am arresting you for the murder of Ronald Burrows and the attempted murder of Marcus Langley."

He nodded to the two constables. As they secured handcuffs around the wrists of Daryl and Vanessa, the DI continued reciting their rights. Then Larry and Tasha led them toward a waiting police car.

I watched them go, their figures silhouetted against the festival lights.

"Nice one, Josie," Einstein said, emerging from beneath the table to jump up beside me.

I looked at the DI, unable to suppress the triumphant grin spreading across my face.

"I hope you got that on record?" I asked him. "Because it would appear you're stuck with me," I said, the satisfaction of being right warming me from the inside.

"I guess I'll have to learn to live with it," he replied, a hint of grudging respect softening his usually stern expression. He held out his hand, the gesture an unexpected acknowledgment of my contribution.

I stood up and shook his hand, feeling oddly formal but pleased by this small victory. His grip was firm and brief, professional but not unfriendly.

"Good evening, Ms Appleton," he said as he turned to walk away. After a few steps, he paused and looked back. "That bit about I couldn't catch a cold..."

"Oh, that," I said quickly, feeling a flush of embarrassment. "That was to put them more at ease. To get them on my side."

"Yes, right," he said, his tone suggesting he didn't believe me for a second. "Thought so."

With a final nod, he walked to his car, his posture once again impeccably straight.

As soon as he was gone, Tom and Sally bounded over to the table, faces alight with excitement. Murphy trotted beside them, tail wagging as if he too understood the significance of what had happened.

"You did it," Tom exclaimed. Without warning, he lifted me off the floor in an exuberant hug, spinning me around.

The unexpected gesture left me momentarily breathless, and Sally speechless.

"I don't know how you did it," Tom continued, lowering me to the ground again. "You are full of surprises, Josie Appleton," he said, his eyes crinkling at the corners with genuine admiration.

Einstein hopped onto the table, his tail held high with pride. "You don't know the half of it," he said, his voice purring with smug satisfaction. "Your grandmother would have been proud."

A warm glow spread through me, as if Beatrix herself had whispered her approval.

Jamie walked over, looking somewhere between impressed and bewildered.

"Well done," he said. "That has to be the fastest solving of a murder I've ever seen."

At that moment, Percy hurtled past, almost dragging Charlie, who was nearly airborne, his little legs scrambling to keep up.

"I heard from Eva!" he shouted. "They've released her. I'm going to pick her up from the police station."

"That's great news," I called back.

Tomorrow, I knew there would be paperwork, and no doubt some pointed questions from DI Holloway about my methods, but tonight, surrounded by smiles, tail wags and the knowledge that the truth had found its way out, it all felt entirely worthwhile.

Chapter 26

I'D HAD PRECISELY TWO hours' sleep.

After giving a brief statement to Jamie Waverley, Tom had driven me home. Neither of us could quite believe I'd solved a murder involving cyanide, muffins and Morris dancers, and we talked all the way back.

However, I'd barely slipped the key in the front door before DI Holloway and Jamie were pulling in to search Daryl King's room.

They found the cyanide tucked in his suitcase, neatly wedged between a bag of peppermint creams and his spare Green Stags polo shirt, and the sun was rising by the time Holloway stepped outside, only to be pursued with surprising agility by Mr Tuppyhead, who appeared to have taken a dislike to the detective's shiny shoes.

There didn't seem much sense in going to bed by then, so I'd dozed in the chair. Sometime during the night, Einstein had curled up on my lap, and I'd woken to his whiskers brushing my cheek and the blare of the alarm on my phone going off.

To my surprise, and relief, breakfast ran surprisingly smoothly. Paula, calm and capable in her *Queen of Porridge* apron, took the lead while I handled tea and coffee duty.

The Crimson Bells were nursing hangovers and blistered feet. The Green Stags, though victorious, were subdued, and the chair where Daryl King should have sat remained conspicuously empty.

Still, one by one, they all said how much they'd loved their stay at Briarwood Gables.

I wasn't sure whether to laugh or cry.

Tom turned up shortly after breakfast to help the guests with their luggage, moving with surprising speed for someone who'd spent all night on a murder investigation.

We stood together on the front path as the last car rumbled down the drive.

He exhaled beside me. "Well, that's us officially folk-dancer-free." He grinned. "I know I'd expected trouble, but I didn't think one of them would commit actual murder."

I nodded. "But there's no blood on the carpet, some five-star reviews, and the goat only chased one detective. I'd call that a win."

As I turned back inside, my eye landed on the hall table.

Gary's envelope.

I picked it up slowly.

Tom frowned. "Everything alright?"

"They're my divorce papers," I said.

Tom started to speak, thought better of it, then tried again. "Do you want some company?"

"I'll want a lift to the post-box," I quipped.

"I'll feed the animals, and I'll drive you," he said, with a level of enthusiasm that made me smile in spite of myself.

Tom headed off towards his caravan and I shut the front door.

Then I glanced at the grandfather clock and my heart sank.

The hands pointed to half past ten. Thirty minutes from now.

Not something else going wrong?

Before I processed this, Paula popped her head out of the kitchen.

"All tidy in there," she told me. "And there's still some egg and bacon, and tea in the pot, if you fancy it."

I smiled at her gratefully. "Thank you so much for all your help," I said. "I couldn't have managed without you."

"Well, I couldn't have solved a murder," said Paula. "You were amazing."

I pulled her into a hug, and, after she'd gone, I carried the divorce papers into the kitchen. I set them on the table, beside the breakfast things Paula had left.

But as I settled in, my phone buzzed.

Kim's face flashed on the screen. Juno and Ivy were peeping over her shoulder. Their hair was tousled, and they were still wearing their pyjamas.

"Hi, sweethearts," I said, smiling even before I'd pressed answer.

"Nana!" the twins chorused.

"You're calling early." I blinked against the sudden wave of emotion that hit me.

"It's nearly seven," Ivy protested, bouncing up and down behind her mother. "And Mummy couldn't wait to know how you've got on with your guests."

"Did they like staying in your house?" Juno chimed in.

"They loved it," I told them. "And my friend Paula made them a yummy breakfast."

Ivy's eyes lit up. "Did anything funny happen?" she asked hopefully.

I grinned. "Well... Agatha the goose stole a pocket watch from one of the guests. Poor Tom had to chase her all over the garden to get it back like a scene straight out of a silly cartoon."

The twins collapsed into delighted giggles.

"And then," I continued, warming to my story, "Mr Tuppy-head, the goat, chased DI Holloway all the way to his car. You would have laughed if you'd seen him running in his smart suit."

"I wish I'd been there to see that," Ivy squealed.

Kim, however, had gone very still.

Her eyes narrowed.

"Right, girls," she said, shooing the twins away. "Time to get yourselves dressed."

She turned back to the screen and fixed me with a hard stare.

"Mum, why was there a detective in your garden?"

I hesitated, watching the steam curl up over my teacup.

Given the transparency I'd promised, I had to tell her.

"There was one minor hiccup with the weekend," I admitted.

Kim's eyes narrowed. "What kind of hiccup?"

"There was... a murder."

Her mouth dropped open.

"But don't worry," I rushed on. "I solved it."

"I'm sorry! What did you say?"

I took a steadying sip of tea.

"One of the judges for the Morris dancing competition was poisoned," I explained. "But I figured it out. It was the leader of the Green Stags Morris dance troupe who was staying in the blue room."

"The murderer was staying in Briarwood Gables!"

"Yes, but the judge wasn't killed here. I mean, what are the odds of two murders happening in one B&B?"

Kim stared at me. "What's the odds there were two murders in Briarvale at all? It looks such a pretty, sleepy little place but...

well, do you think you should consider moving somewhere less... murdery?"

"Nonsense," I replied. "This sort of thing happens everywhere."

Kim groaned. "Yes, but..."

"Your father sent me divorce papers," I blurted out.

In the interest of honesty, she had to know.

It wasn't the smoothest way to break the news, but at least it stopped her mid-rant about Briarvale's body count.

There was a silence.

Longer this time.

"Oh, Mum," she said softly. "I'm so sorry."

I tucked my fingers round my teacup, hoping Kim didn't notice the slight tremble.

"Nothing to be sorry about, love," I said. "Honestly, it's the nicest thing your father's done for years."

Kim gave a quick sniff. "Are you sure you're okay?"

"Well, I am tired," I admitted. "Murder investigations are rather draining."

Kim's eyes glistened a little. "I'm glad you told me about the divorce."

I smiled, relief flooding through me. Not just because Kim knew the truth about everything and seemed OK with it, but because I was OK with it, too.

"I'm going to sign the papers and Tom's giving me a lift to the post-box as soon as I've finished my tea," I said.

There. All truths told.

Well... all except for the biggest one that affected us all. The one about witches and spells, and the legacy which she and her girls would one day carry.

That was a story I wasn't ready to say out loud.

Not yet.

"OK, but promise me you'll have at least one weekend where nobody dies," said Kim.

I laughed, shaking my head at the absurdity of my life.

"I'll do my best."

When the call ended, I pulled the envelope closer and slipped the papers out. The pen sat beside me, waiting.

And then came a knock on the front door.

Eva Henshaw stood on the step. Her hair was neatly clipped back as always, but her eyes were rimmed with dark circles. I guess she hadn't slept much either.

In her hand was a small bouquet of cottage garden flowers, beautifully wrapped in pale pink tissue paper.

"Josie," she said, and there was a warmth in her voice I'd never known from her before. "I heard what you did, how you revealed the real murderers. I wanted to stop by and thank you for seeing the truth and saying it when no one else did."

"Eva," I gasped, surprised but pleased. "I didn't expect..."

But she cut me off. "It was the least I could do." She held out the bouquet. "They're from my garden. I really am most terribly grateful."

Tears pricked my eyes as I took the blooms. "They're beautiful."

Eva sniffed. "I'm good at flower arranging," she said briskly, "no matter what Ronald Burrows used to think."

"Do you want to come in?" I asked.

Eva shook her head. "Can't stay. Too much to process right now. But listen, Josie, if there's ever anything you need, you only have to ask."

And with that, she turned and walked back down the path to where Percy was waiting in the car, her head held high.

Einstein, who'd been perched on the stairs observing our visitor, padded silently to my side.

"Wow," he said. "Approval from Eva Henshaw. I didn't think there was such a thing. I'd say you are an official member of the village of Briarvale now, Josie Appleton."

I carried the flowers into the kitchen with a huge smile on my face. The divorce papers were still on the table. Without the slightest hesitation, I picked up the pen and signed my name with a flourish.

And at that exact moment, the grandfather clock began to chime, bright and joyful, like I'd never heard before.

It was ten-thirty.

Einstein jumped. "Not heard that in a while," he chortled.

"Was that... for me signing the papers?" I gasped.

"I'd say so," said Einstein.

"So, it wasn't a warning. More a... celebration. A letting-go."

Einstein hopped lightly onto the chair beside me and nudged my arm. "I told you, the clock doesn't only herald doom."

I smiled.

"Sometimes," he said, curling into a purring ball of fur and whiskers, "it marks the start of something new."

I nodded. "And if that *something* happens to include a few more mysteries, well... I'm ready."

·✦ · ✰ ·✦· ✦ · ✶ ·

Josie's ready for cinnamon buns and snowflakes, not corpses under the Christmas tree. Join her for a festive whodunit in *Christmas, Clues and Killers*.

· ✦ · ✮ · ◀✦ · ★ · ★ ·

If you loved Josie and Einstein's story, you can help other readers solve the crimes in Briarvale by *leaving a review*. Just a couple of lines saying what you liked about the book will be great.

· ✦ · ✮ · ◀✦ · ★ · ★ ·

Curious how murder and magic first tangled in Briarvale? Join Josie as she dives into her grandmother Beatrix's diary and uncovers the truth. Download the free prequel, *Destiny, Diaries and Death* and uncover the secrets that started it all.

www.bellacolby.com

WITCHY @ 50

BELLA COLBY
books

Printed in Dunstable, United Kingdom

66017941R00127